THE EARL'S MASQUERADE

The Earl's Masquerade

Published in June, 2018 by Harington House Press,
Temecula, CA

ISBN: 9781732459809

Cover design by Kimberly Westrope

Printed in the U.S.A.

Dedication

To

Steve Moulton,

a friend and a gentleman

The Earl's Masquerade

Acknowledgements

Thank you to my lovely BETA readers, Carolee Moore, Kathy Heinrichs, Lisa McConnell, Angie Anderson, Jenna Anderson, and Julie Shilling. Your input and ideas are always very helpful and much appreciated. You're the best of friends and sisters. I love you ladies.

A special thank you to my British BETA, Helena Fairfax for invaluable guidance and suggestions. You are a true blessing!

Thank you to DJ, Steven, and David Garrett for inspiration.

As always, thank you to my friends and family for their continued and abundant support and encouragement.

Thank you to all my fabulous Facebook author/friends, who are always supportive and such sweet, wonderful people. I am happy to be part of such a lovely talented group of writers.

Lastly, but never least, thank you, Jesus Christ, my Lord and Savior, for giving me the love of writing and the gift that enables me to do what I love.

Other Titles by This Author

Inspirational Romance

BROTHER'S KEEPER

Poetry

DANCING ON BORDERS

THE PRINTS OF ALL MY DAYS

THE EARL'S MASQUERADE

Kimberly Westrope

HARINGTON HOUSE PRESS
Temecula, Ca

CHAPTER ONE

"Hath the pearl less whiteness
Because of its birth?
Hath the violet less brightness
For growing near earth."
from *Desmond's Song*

"Ouch!"

Miss Catherine Elmsworth flinched when the seamstress accidently poked her with a pin as she gathered up the seam at Catherine's waist. She glanced over at the velvet settee where her aunt Margaret sat primly, just in time to see the slight scowl on her aunt's face.

"Do stand still, Catherine, or we'll never get this fitting finished."

Pulling herself up straight again, Catherine pouted, "I'm trying to Auntie, but it is hard to stand still when one is being poked repeatedly with sharp objects." She kept her voice light and tried not to glare at Mrs. Booth, the seamstress, who managed a "tsk" despite the several pins she still held between her lips.

Removing the pins, Mrs. Booth smiled brightly up at Catherine. "There now, my lady, all finished." She reached out to help Catherine down from her perch on the large ottoman. Turning to Lady Margaret Hathaway, she asked, "Will the young lady be trying on the dress from yesterday, my lady?"

"Oh yes, let us see the effects of your handiwork, Mrs. Booth," Aunt Margaret replied.

Catherine sighed. It seemed to her they'd been at this tedious task for hours, and she'd had enough. She desperately wanted to change back into her old gown and go home.

"Emily," called Mrs. Booth. "Please come and help Miss Elmsworth out of this gown, and into the green one from yesterday." A young woman came out from the back of the dressmaker's shop and escorted Catherine to the changing room. "And do take care not to poke her with the pins when you remove the dress, dear," Mrs. Booth added, wryly.

Several moments later, Catherine came to stand in front of the three-sided, full length mirror. The dress was gorgeous. The emerald green silk fell in soft folds from her hips to the floor. The color blended beautifully with her medium auburn hair and fair complexion, and made her green eyes look even greener.

"Oh, my dear girl," gushed Aunt Margaret, rising from the settee and coming to stand beside Catherine. "You look absolutely stunning," she said, looking at Catherine in the mirror. Her smile faltered slightly as she gazed at Catherine's reflection. Wiping away a stray tear, she said, "You look so much like your dear mother, Catherine. How I wish she were here to see the beautiful young woman you've become. She and your father would be so proud."

"Oh Auntie, no tears now," replied Catherine, giving her aunt a hug. "I do miss them, of course, but you have become so dear to me, so like a mother, that I sometimes forget you haven't always been so."

"Yes, I too sometimes forget you are not my daughter by birth. These six years since their passing, I have watched you grow and change from a child to a woman, and it has been my great honor to have the privilege of caring for you, dear." Lady Hathaway let out a soft sigh. "I remember your mother at the same age you are now, getting ready for her first season. It seems like only yesterday."

Twirling in her dress and turning to look over her shoulder at the back of the gown, Catherine smiled at her aunt. "And I wager you were the nicest big sister, helping her get all prettied up for the balls, and giving her pointers on how to bewitch all the single gentlemen."

"Well, I was already a married woman by then, so I suppose I did have some experience in that area," she replied with a chuckle. "But it did not take much tutoring with your mother. She had all the young men wrapped around her finger from the moment she stepped into the ballroom at her first ball." Lady Hathaway smiled fondly, her memories coming to life in that moment. "None of the others stood a chance, though, once she'd laid eyes on Jerome Elmsworth. Lizzy was smitten from the moment she saw him across the room. I knew, watching them dancing together, there would be no one else for either of them."

"There never was, either," replied Catherine, wistfully. "They were as much in love on the day they died as they were on the day they married, of that I am sure."

"Yes, that is true. I never saw a man more completely devoted to his wife and family. Even my dear William, I dare say. Though he was quite a wonderful husband and provider, he was never the romantic type like your father was."

"I remember him sitting by the parlor fire in the evenings, reading poetry to Mother and me, though I suspect it was more for Mother than for my benefit," Catherine giggled. "I learned from him how a real gentleman should behave. I hope I am as lucky as my mother was in finding such a gentleman."

"I am certain you will find someone equally as handsome and as charming, dear. Now, let's get you out of that dress. We'll stop at the tea shop for some refreshments before we head back home."

Catherine was exhausted by the time they arrived back home at Aunt Margaret's. She excused herself to her aunt and went up to her room to rest a bit. Lying back on the huge four poster bed, Catherine sank into the plush softness of the coverlet, painted with pink roses so lovely you could almost smell them. Catherine took in a deep breath as if she really could smell their sweet fragrance. Taking another deep breath, her thoughts drifted to her parents as she dozed off to sleep.

The Elmsworths were not nearly as well off as their high borne relations were. Most of Catherine's mother's family believed that Lady Elizabeth Worthington had married far below her class when she married Jerome Elmsworth, whom many of them still considered to be a mere tradesman even though Jerome had managed, through stringent saving and wise investment, to become a man of means and a land owner of quite a large estate.

There were some, of course, who were happy Lizzy had found love, no matter how wealthy her husband was or how he had acquired his wealth. Jerome Elmsworth was every bit the gentleman his peers were and, truth be told, more of a gentleman than most. Elizabeth's older sister, Margaret, was one of the few who welcomed Jerome into the family with open arms, glad her little sister had found true love and happiness with a man who adored her and treated her so well.

Jerome never forgot his roots, despite his great fortune. He was a humble man, and never flaunted his wealth. During his time as a tradesman, it was evident by his work ethic that Jerome was a man of honor. As young as he was, he quickly gained a reputation as a man of integrity and one who treated everyone fairly in his dealings with them. Even members of the wealthy upper class, who had occasion to do business with him, held him in high esteem.

One evening just before dusk, as he was headed home from his shop, the twenty-one-year old Jerome happened upon two men accosting a young woman in what appeared to be a sinister manner. Jerome became so enraged that adrenaline poured through him, giving him a sudden bravery and strength as he approached them, pulling the men from the young woman and threatening them with such conviction that they gave up and ran away. Jerome gently helped the young woman steady herself.

"Are you all right?" he asked. "Did they harm you?"

"I am fine," the lovely blonde replied. She looked to be a year or two younger than Jerome. "They were mostly just talk, trying to frighten me. I don't believe they actually meant to do me harm, though you certainly did some harm to them." She smiled timidly as her cheeks flushed a light pink.

"Yes, I'm afraid I did," Jerome blushed slightly as well. "When I saw that you seemed to be in danger, I did not take the time to ask their intent. Nor did I care what their intent was. What they were doing was unacceptable regardless." The anger coursed threw him once more. "No man should treat a lady thus."

Jerome looked into her deep blue eyes. "Forgive me for prying, my lady, but why are you out walking about alone at dusk? Surely you are aware that it is not safe practice, nor is it acceptable for a young lady such as yourself to be out and about without at least her maid to accompany her."

The young woman looked at her feet sheepishly for a moment before answering. "You are right, of course, and I do not make a habit of doing such as this, but I had just left my friend Lady Morgan's home just down the street there, and it being such a short distance to my own home, I thought I would be fine walking it alone." She peered up at Jerome. "Obviously, I was wrong. I am glad you happened along when you did." She put her hand out toward Jerome. "I am Lady Julia Whitcomb, and I thank you for your assistance."

Taking her gloved hand in his, Jerome bent over it with a deep bow. "It was my pleasure to be of assistance, my lady. My name is Jerome Elmsworth, and if I may be so bold, I would like to offer my further assistance and walk you to your door."

"That would be so kind of you, though I'd hate to trouble you further, Mr. Elmsworth."

"No trouble at all Lady Julia. I would consider it an honor to escort you." Jerome held out his arm, which Julia gratefully placed her hand on, and they proceeded to her home.

Jerome was shocked to find out Lady Julia Whitcomb was the daughter of His Grace, The

Duke of Farcourt. The Duke was extremely grateful to Jerome for coming to his daughter's rescue and seeing her safely home. Jerome was invited to stay and dine with the Duke and his family, where he was introduced to Lady Julia's brother, Corbett. The two young men got on well, conversing throughout the meal. Finding they had many common interests, they became quite companionable and were soon the best of friends.

No one in the Duke's family seemed to notice that Jerome was not of their social standing. He always dressed and behaved impeccably and was readily accepted into their home and into their lives as if he were one of them. Granted, His Grace was known for his kind regard of the lower classes despite his lofty position. Many of the *haut ton* looked down their noses at him because of his fondness for those of lower means. However, The Duke of Farcourt was also known to be a fair and generous man, and many regarded him very highly as a man of great character and integrity, therefore accepting into their peerage anyone whom His Grace deemed fit to dwell among them.

It was in this manner that young Jerome began to be accepted into many of the homes of London's high society where he was found to be quite a fine young gentleman. Before long, many of the mothers of London began parading their daughters before Jerome, considering him to be quite acceptable as husband material.

There were some, of course, who still considered him to be far beneath their standards, but despite his lack of immense wealth, Jerome did manage to build up a nice bank account for himself, and there was no denying his charm. Some would even say it was his very likable personality alone that garnered him invitations to so many of the most prestigious social gatherings. Jerome always behaved in the most gentlemanly manner, thus keeping his fine reputation intact.

Of course, being the best friend of The Duke of Farcourt's son, and practically a member of the Duke's family, definitely increased Jerome's appeal. So it was, that he found himself invited to party after party during the London season of his twenty-first year. It was at one such gathering that Jerome Elmsworth first laid eyes on the most beautiful woman he had ever seen.

Though he stood clear across the room from the main entrance, Jerome's gaze was immediately drawn to the young woman, dressed in brilliant blue, as she entered the room. He was so entranced that he completely abandoned the conversation he'd been having with his friends until, noticing his sudden lack of participation in the discussion, they began cajoling him, trying to see what it was that had drawn his attention away.

There, in all her fresh young beauty, stood Lady Elizabeth Worthington, the woman who would one day become Mrs. Jerome Elmsworth.

A week later, Cathcrine found herself once again at the seamstress's shop, back up on the wide ottoman, being prodded and poked. She and Aunt Margaret had been there nearly every day for the past week. Between these sessions with the dressmaker, and the endless hours she'd spent in dance instruction, Catherine was exhausted. She let her shoulders slump as a heavy sigh escaped her lips.

"Auntie Margaret, must I endure this torture for a minute more?" Catherine pleaded with her aunt. "How many new dresses *does* one need for season in London? I don't see how I can possibly wear them all unless we go to a ball every night."

"Patience, my dear," said her aunt. "You will be thankful you endured all this when all eyes are on you at every event we attend this season. And, trust me, there will be many invitations. Perhaps not every night, but at least several a week, I would wager."

"Several a week?" Catherine let out another sigh. "It tires me, just thinking of it."

Catherine was not overly fond of socializing. She was pleasant enough whenever she and her aunt had guests, or if they were invited to a gathering at a friend's house, but she didn't exactly go out of her way to be social. She preferred to stay at home, preferably in her aunt's large library where she often lost herself amongst the many tomes. More often than not, Aunt Margaret or one of her house staff would find Catherine curled up in one of the big comfy chairs oblivious to the world around her, so engrossed was she in the worlds of the books she devoured.

"You will change that way of thinking as soon as you have attended your first ball," Lady Margaret replied. "I am confident you will soon enough become the belle of all the balls, and have many young men vying for your attentions." Her aunt let out a little chuckle, as she mused over the idea, which made Catherine even less enthused about going to any social gatherings, balls or otherwise.

Thankfully, this would be her last fitting before the start of the season. Her aunt had really gone all out and had ordered twelve new ball gowns made for Catherine's coming out season, despite all of Catherine's protestations as to the necessity of such extravagance. Aunt Margaret had always been a bit extreme in pampering Catherine in the time her niece had lived with her. Lady Hathaway had no children of her own, and being a widow of some means, she thoroughly enjoyed spoiling her niece when it struck her fancy to do so.

Less than a week later, Catherine received her first invitation. There was to be a ball at the home of Lord and Lady Meriwether, The Earl and Countess of Hawthorne, to start off the season. Lady Hathaway clapped her hands together with glee as Catherine read the invitation to her over breakfast. Catherine held in a groan. *So, it begins,* she thought as she laid aside the invitation and took up her glass of juice, averting her eyes away from her aunt's scrutiny.

The Earl's Masquerade

CHAPTER TWO

"I give thee all – I can no more –
Though poor the offering be;
My heart and lute are all the store
That I can bring to thee.
A lute whose gentle song reveal
The soul of love full well;
And, better by far, a heart that feels
Much more than lute could tell."

from *My Heart And A Lute*

The evening of the ball, as her lady's maid, Abby, helped her dress in one of her new gowns, Catherine tried to keep her spirits up. The gown was light blue with ivory lace adorning the bodice and sleeves. As the maid hooked a lovely pearl necklace around her slender neck, Catherine practiced her pleasant face in the mirror. How would she ever be able to maintain that look for an entire evening?

Abby was just putting the finishing touches on Catherine's curls adding several small pink roses, when Aunt Margaret tapped on the door and entered the room.

"Heavens!" she exclaimed, her eyes alight with joy. "You look lovely, Catherine." She placed her hands gently on her niece's shoulders, meeting her gaze in the mirror. "Are we ready to greet the hordes of young, eligible men that await?"

Smiling up at her aunt, Catherine rose from her seat, taking her aunt's hand in her own. "I am as ready as I will ever be, Auntie. Lead the way."

Stepping out of the carriage ahead of her aunt, Catherine glanced around the large drive in front of the Lord and Lady Hawthorne's magnificent home and was struck by the quantity of carriages she saw lined up the length of the long drive. The numerous carriages bespoke of the crowd of people that awaited her inside. Her stomach a ball of nerves, Catherine followed her aunt up to the main door of the Hawthorne mansion, where they were greeted by one of several doormen. He took their names and announced them to the assembled group in the foyer.

Hesitant to enter the fray before her, Catherine held back a bit when her aunt moved further into the room. She gazed at the splendor around her, her eyes wide and her mouth slightly open in awe and wonder. Her aunt's home was, of course, very well appointed and beautiful in an understated way. Aunt Margaret liked lovely things as much as any woman, but she wasn't one for extravagance. The gleaming gold and crystal shining all around her in the huge entryway told Catherine that the Earl and Countess Hawthorne did indeed enjoy fine things. She grew excited to see the grand ballroom.

Just as she took a small step forward, something collided with her, nearly knocking her off her feet. A strong hand grabbed her arm, keeping her from toppling over.

"Pardon me, I…" Catherine heard the male voice falter.

Gathering herself up to rights, Catherine met the stalled gaze of brown eyes the color of a newborn fawn, eyes fringed with the longest lashes she had ever seen on any man. For the briefest of moments, neither of them spoke.

He broke the moment when he suddenly removed his hand as if it had been scorched by fire. Bowing slightly as he stared at his feet, the young man mumbled, "In my haste, I did not see you there, my lady."

He raised his eyes just a bit to meet hers again. Catherine found her own eyes drawn to the man's full shapely lips as he spoke. She noticed that his hair was styled differently than was the fashion of the day. His was a bit longer than most men wore theirs, and it was held at the nape of his neck with a black ribbon. A long wisp of it had come loose from the ribbon and now gently caressed the side of his face. Catherine at once felt the strange desire to reach out and touch it. Restraining herself, she brought her eyes back to his.

"Forgive me," he said in a barely audible whisper as he turned and rushed off.

Catherine stood speechless. Aunt Margaret, who had noticed the lack of her niece's presence beside her, had turned back just in time to witness the incident. She returned to Catherine's side.

"Such a rude young man, rushing about willy-nilly, bumping into innocent bystanders like that," Lady Hathaway huffed. Taking her niece's arm, she guided her forward, adding, "Come along, Catherine."

Catherine went with her aunt, but not before casting a backwards glance down the hall in the direction the young man had gone. She looked back over her shoulder just as he turned to look back over his, and for a second time, their eyes met for a brief moment. He quickly turned away, but not before Catherine caught the small smile that came to his lips. It lightened her heart and eased her nervous stomach in a strange sort of way. Puzzling over it, she nearly stumbled again as her aunt led her into the great ballroom.

As Garrett rushed down the hall and hurriedly returned to his seat with the orchestra, his friend Adam, also a violinist, glanced up from tuning his instrument. Noticing his friend's flushed and flustered appearance, Adam asked, "What is ailing you, Garrett? You look as though you've had a fright." He chuckled softly. "Either that, or you have imbibed in too much drink, which I know, my friend, you would never do."

Garrett would not meet his friend's eye. "Nothing...I'm fine", he answered dismissively, turning away from his friend as he checked the tuning of his instrument.

Shrugging, Adam turned his attention back to his own instrument. They both settled into their seats as the Master of Ceremonies began the evening's entertainment.

As the music began, Garrett took a deep breath and closed his eyes. He lifted his bow and began playing. His shoulders relaxed as his fingers caressed the strings of his violin while the bow moved effortlessly over their surface. When Garrett played his violin, he lost himself in the music. He felt as one with his instrument as the glorious notes surrounded him.

As he played, the image of a beautiful young woman surfaced at the back of his mind. Her auburn hair and green eyes became clearer as Garrett played. Cursing himself, Garrett pushed the image out of his thoughts and forced himself to stay focused on the music. The image would not relent. The beautiful young woman he had nearly bowled over would not let him be.

Who is she? he wondered. He had a sudden desire to know her and to know everything about her. *Wait, what is wrong with me?* he asked himself. He'd never had such a strong reaction to any woman before. Despite his best efforts, he couldn't shake her image from his thoughts.

When he had grabbed hold of her arm to keep her from falling, his fingers filled with a sudden heat as if he had touched a hot coal. And when her emerald eyes held his, he felt his face flush with the same heat. He'd been so stunned, he nearly ran from her presence, but not before that one glance back over his shoulder. Seeing that she, too, had turned back to watch him go, he'd smiled, an unexplainable feeling of happiness enveloping him.

Adam cleared his throat next to Garrett, and when Garrett looked over, his friend looked back questioningly. Returning a slight shake of his head, Garrett forced himself to concentrate on the music. He was able to get through the first piece without any more distraction from the lovely young lady.

The two ladies made their way around the outer edges of the room, Aunt Margaret leading the way and introducing Catherine to every clutch of people they encountered along the way. Catherine's eyes scanned the room, looking for a particular young man. So many of the men were dressed in similar fashion, it was hard to distinguish one from another. Surely, though, his unique hair style would cause him to stand out from the others, if nothing else.

"Lord and Lady Mosbey, how wonderful to see you," Margaret greeted an older couple. "It has been such a long time since we have all been at the same gathering. And young Harry, isn't it?" she asked turning to their son who accompanied them. "I dare say, Harry, you have grown into quite a handsome young man," she gushed. "Please allow me to introduce my niece, Miss Catherine Elmsworth. Catherine, these are my good friends, Lord Jonathan Fatham, The Earl of Mosbey, and Lady Madeline Fatham, The Countess of Mosbey. And this is their son, Harry, The Viscount Moreland."

"It is a pleasure to meet you both, My Lord, Lady Mosbey. My aunt has often spoken of you."

Turning her attention to the young man her aunt had introduced as The Viscount Moreland, Catherine greeted him as well. "Lord Moreland, it is an honor to make your acquaintance." Her aunt was correct in calling him handsome for he was indeed. His blonde curls and blue eyes were quite captivating. He was tall and held himself well, in a relaxed manner. His straight nose and strong chin gave him an elegant, almost regal air.

Taking her gloved hand as he bowed, young Lord Moreland replied, "I assure you, the honor is mine, Miss Elmsworth," he said, releasing her hand. "And I would be doubly honored if you would agree to dance the first waltz with me."

"Of course, my lord. That would be lovely," replied Catherine. "Thank you for asking."

"It's so good of you to offer, Lord Moreland," said Lady Hathaway, "as Catherine has no male relative present to waltz with her, and a young woman should not have to sit out the waltzes at her first ball due to lack of a partner. With our families being close friends, I believe it would be most acceptable for you to accompany her."

"I am glad to be of service, Lady Hathaway." Smiling at Catherine, he added, "I will look forward to it, Miss Elmsworth."

At that moment, two other young men joined the group. "Good evening, Lord Mosbey, Lady Mosbey, Moreland," they greeted the Earl, his Countess, and Harry. They were obviously already well-acquainted with Harry and his parents. Eyeing Catherine, the taller of the two asked, "And who have we here, Moreland? Have you been keeping this beautiful young lady all to yourself?"

Lord Mosbey spoke. "Allow me to present Lady Margaret Hathaway and her niece, Miss Catherine Elmsworth. Ladies, these are my son's friends from school, The Honorable James Worth, and The Honorable Arthur Fellows." Both young men nodded in acknowledgement.

The shorter and more handsome of the two, Mr. Fellows, turned to Lady Margaret. He smiled, first at Margaret, then at Catherine, taking each offered hand and bowing to each of them. "It is a pleasure to meet you, Lady Hathaway. Miss Elmsworth."

Arthur stepped forward and spoke directly to Catherine. "Miss Elmsworth, may I have the pleasure of your company for the supper dance?" he asked boldly. "That is assuming you've not yet pledged it to someone else."

"I have not, and you may, Mr. Fellows," answered Catherine with a demure smile.

"Now that we've been properly introduced, I must tell you that I look forward to furthering our acquaintance," he stated rather smugly.

Well he's quite the princox, isn't he, assuming I would want to further such an acquaintance? Catherine thought to herself while presenting Arthur with the sweetest smile she could muster. *A bit too pompous for my taste.*

Mr. Worth came up beside Catherine. Turning to look at her, he said "Perhaps, Miss Elmsworth, you might also consider saving a dance for me?"

Catherine eyed him. *This one is an altogether different sort*, she thought. *Definitely less sure of himself, and more humble.* "Why yes, Mr. Worth, it would be my great pleasure," she answered enthusiastically and just loud enough for Arthur to hear.

The dances settled, conversation moved on to other things, things of which Catherine had no interest whatsoever. Only half listening to the conversation that buzzed around her, Catherine casually let her eyes wander around the room, hoping her aunt and the others wouldn't notice her lack of attention.

Her eyes brushed past the small orchestra seated at the far end of the room, then quickly returned as she caught sight of one of the violinists, whose dark brown hair was gathered at the nape of his neck with a black ribbon. She couldn't see his face, but Catherine was certain there was only one person in the room tonight wearing that hair style. It had to be him.

Needing a closer look, Catherine discreetly disengaged herself from the group and moved toward the musician's seating area. She stopped a few feet away from where the violinist sat. Pretending to inspect the large potted fern next to her, Catherine peeked over at the musicians. From this vantage point, she could see the face of the young violinist. Yes! It was him!

Oh my, but he is handsome, Catherine murmured to herself as she gazed at him, hypnotized. Eyes closed, he swayed gently as he played. He seemed completely absorbed in the music. Catherine quite forgot herself and where she was as she stood watching him.

Suddenly, as if he had sensed her there, his eyes opened and fixed on hers. She saw the tiny smile come to his lips as he gave her the tiniest nod of his head. Catherine felt the heat rise in her cheeks as she smiled back at him.

The spell was broken when Aunt Margaret's shrill, "Catherine!" invaded. "There you are, dear. I got quite worried when you seemed to have disappeared into thin air." Noticing her niece's flushed cheeks and the quick glance toward the musicians, Lady Hathaway followed Catherine's line of sight and saw the young violinist quickly drop his gaze.

"Whatever are you doing, Catherine, lingering here in the corner instead of mingling?" Margaret harrumphed. "This is completely inappropriate behavior and will not do at all." She took hold of Catherine's arm, pulling her away. "The waltz will begin soon, and you've promised it to Lord Moreland."

With a sigh, Catherine let herself be led away once more from the young man.

Moments later, she was joined by Lord Moreland, as the waltz began. Catherine purposefully led him to an open spot as close to the orchestra as she could get. Each time she circled around to face the orchestra, she found the young violinist's eyes on her. Her face heated again under his constant gaze, though she tried to convince herself it was from the exertion of the dance. Harry didn't seem to notice Catherine's straying eyes. When the dance was finished, she curtsied, her eyes once again on the violinist. He tipped his head slightly, giving her the most beatific smile. Noticing the slight dimples in his cheeks, Catherine thought she had never seen a lovelier man.

Harry returned Catherine to her Aunt Margaret, where she found an acquaintance of hers, Lady Meredith Covington, conversing with her aunt. He then excused himself and re-joined his friends.

"Meredith, how lovely to see you!" Catherine said, "I was beginning to wonder if I would see anyone I knew here tonight."

"Oh, but you seem to have made at least one new friend." Meredith answered slyly. "Wasn't that Lord Moreland you were just dancing with?"

"Yes, Lord Moreland and I were introduced earlier this evening, and I promised him a waltz. He's a very good dancer."

"And handsome, as well, is he not?"

Aunt Margaret answered, "Oh yes, he has grown into quite a handsome young man, though he may be just a bit too serious," she frowned. "Still, he would make a fine husband for either one of you girls." She eyed them both pointedly. "Now, if you'll excuse me, I am in need of some refreshment."

Meredith turned to Catherine conspiratorially. "And you, Catherine, do you find Lord Moreland handsome?"

"Yes, I supposed he would be considered a handsome man," Catherine agreed.

"And yet your eyes keep searching out someone else, do they not?" Meredith teased.

Catherine turned to face the orchestra once more, searching. There, through the crowd, her eyes found him. *Who was this man who seemed to have cast a spell over her?* She was mesmerized by him and yearned to know more of him. If only she could ask someone.

"Who is it you are so enchanted with?" asked Meredith, trying to see where Catherine's gaze fell.

"There," Catherine nodded her head in the direction of the orchestra. "Do you see the young violinist in the first row of the orchestra?"

"What? The violinist?" Meredith laughed. "You cannot be serious, Catherine. Please tell me you are toying with me." She saw the seriousness on Catherine's face. "A musician?"

"Who is he?" Catherine whispered, more to herself than to her friend.

"No one of consequence," Meredith replied, dismissively. "Have you met Lord Harington, yet?"

Catherine shook her head slightly, tearing her eyes away from the musician.

"Come then, I must introduce you. Lord Harington is the most eligible bachelor in the room, and the richest. He is also quite pleasing to look at. I am sure you will find him quite charming." She pulled a reluctant Catherine through the crowd.

"Lady Covington, how nice to see you again," the gentleman said as the ladies approached him. He reached his hand out to take Meredith's, bowing low over it. Rising, his eyes fell upon Catherine.

"Lord Harington, always a pleasure to see you," said Meredith. "May I introduce you to an acquaintance of mine, Miss Elmsworth. She is Lady Hathaway's niece. Miss Elmsworth, it is my pleasure to make known to you Lord Brooks Darling, The Earl of Harington."

"Ah yes," Lord Harington replied. "Lady Hathaway has made mention of you to me on a number of occasions," he said, taking Catherine's hand and bowing once more. "It is a pleasure to finally meet you, Miss Elmsworth."

As he righted himself, his gaze held Catherine's for just a moment, long enough for her to notice what pleasant features he had - high cheekbones, a strong chin, and a straight, perfect nose. His eyes were of such a deep blue hue that Catherine momentarily lost herself in them.

Suddenly in their place was a pair of tawny eyes with long, beautiful lashes. Warm eyes gazing back at her so intensely. Catherine shook her head to clear it, smiling at the gentleman before her.

"I must confess I have heard much talk of you as well, my lord," she said. "In fact, I've heard it rumored that you are the most eligible bachelor for miles around," she teased.

Is he blushing? My goodness, did I make the poor man blush? I really do need to take more care with what I say, thought Catherine.

"Well, I don't know about that, Miss Elmsworth, but perhaps it would be to both of our advantages to not judge one another based on the words of others, but by becoming better acquainted with one another ourselves."

"Perhaps you are right, my lord."

"In that pursuit, may I claim the next dance with you, Miss Elmsworth?"

"I would be honored, Lord Harington."

Turning to Meredith, Lord Harington asked, "And you, Lady Covington? May I have the opportunity to dance with you this evening as well?"

"My Lord, nothing would please me more," answered Meredith, beaming up at him.

As the music started for the country dance, Catherine and Lord Harington found their place amongst the dancers. Being much more attentive to her than Lord Moreland had been, the earl made it difficult for Catherine's attention to wander elsewhere, though she did try.

When the dance had finished, Lord Harington escorted Catherine from the dance floor.

"Thank you, Miss Elmsworth," he said, depositing her next to Meredith. "That was quite exhilarating."

Catherine smiled up at him. "It was a pleasure, my lord." She glanced around the room. "And now I fear I must find Mr. Fellows, to whom I have promised the supper dance." Glancing up at him once more, she added, "If you will excuse me," as she rushed off.

Brooks watched her go. Turning to Meredith, he put out his arm for her to take. "Well, Lady Covington, this is our dance. Shall we?"

Unfortunately, the supper dance was a long one. Catherine found herself wishing for it to end almost as soon as it had begun. Mr. Fellows spoke only of himself through the entire course of the dance. It appeared that his own accomplishments were his favorite topic of conversation. Catherine was dreading spending the whole of supper seated next to him. Her spirits were lifted a bit, however, when she found that Lord Moreland would also be present, seated at her other side. Though she had no romantic interest in either of them, she much preferred Harry's company to that of his friend.

CHAPTER THREE

"Ah, well may we hope,
when this short life is gone,
To meet in some world
of more permanent bliss;
For a smile, or a grasp of the hand,
hastening on,
Is all we enjoy of each other in this."
from *And Doth Not A Meeting Like This*

With supper ended, everyone wandered back into the ballroom for the final dances of the evening. Wishing to escape the crowd and the noise for a brief moment, Catherine detoured through the french doors that let out to a paved terrace overlooking the garden. She breathed deeply taking in the fresh air. Tilting her head up a bit, she gazed at the moon. A flash of light suddenly lit the sky, a falling star. Catherine knew immediately what to wish for. She closed her eyes, letting the cool breeze brush over her skin. It felt like a heavenly kiss.

"There is nothing more beautiful than a lass in the moonlight," said a soft male voice behind her. Somehow, it hadn't startled her in the least to hear a strange man's voice come upon her suddenly out here alone in the dark. Yet it wasn't strange at all. In fact, it seemed very familiar. She didn't need to look to know who it was who stood there with her. But she did look.

She turned and found those lovely brown eyes embracing her with longing. Rather than being embarrassed under his intense gaze, Catherine found herself craving it. She wanted to be held by those eyes, and yes by his arms, too, if she were to be honest about it.

"Forgive me, my lady, for being so bold." He dropped his gaze for a moment before raising his eyes to meet hers again. "I saw you come out here, and…I wished to know your name," he said softly. His voice was like warm butter flowing over her. Even from the distance that separated them, she could feel the heat emanating from him.

"Catherine," she spoke barely above a whisper, forgetting all propriety. "My name is Catherine."

"Catherine," he said huskily. "'Tis a beautiful name for a beautiful lady."

Hearing him speak her name, Catherine became aware of his accent. *What was it? Irish? He is an Irishman then?*

Shaking her head to clear it, she attempted to correct her societal blunder. "Um," she faltered, "Miss Elmsworth, my lord"

"Please allow me to introduce myself, Miss Elmsworth," he said with a low bow. "I am Garrett Brennen, and as you have seen and heard, I am a violinist." Offering her a grin, he straightened himself. "At your service."

"Yes, and may I say, you play beautifully," she answered. "I quite enjoyed listening whilst dancing."

"Ah yes, the dancing," he replied with a smirk. "You did seem to be enjoying that. I could see that you were very focused on the dance."

Catherine felt the heat come into her cheeks as he teased her, knowing that he knew full well where her attention had been during those dances.

"Do you enjoy music?" he asked, casually moving a few steps closer to her. They both stood at the edge of the patio, looking out toward the garden.

"Oh yes!" Catherine answered. "I enjoy it very much. Though I don't play, I'm afraid. My aunt encouraged me in that direction as a young girl, but I never quite had the talent for it."

"Do you have a favorite tune?" he asked.

Without hesitation, she answered, "I have always loved "Lady Greensleeves. It is a beautiful love song, but also very sad."

"Yes, I know it well," Garrett replied.

"Do you believe it was really written by Henry the Eighth for Anne Boleyn?" she inquired.

"I'm afraid not. It is my understanding that it was actually written by a Richard Jones in 1580 and was originally called "A Newe Northen Dittye of ye Ladye Greene Sleves," he said, putting on a strong Olde English accent.

Catherine smiled and nodded lightly, impressed with his knowledge of the history of her favorite song.

"It is a nice notion, though, is it not," she asked, "to think that the awful King Henry had a soft side, that he might have actually truly loved someone other than himself?"

"Aye, I must agree with you on that," Garrett replied. "There is no greater notion is there, than the possibility of truly loving and being loved by another?" He turned to her, then, and Catherine again felt the heat of him as his sleeve brushed hers.

She stood speechless before him, as thoughts raced through her mind. *All this talk of love,* she mused. *Is that what this is all about? Could these strange feelings I am feeling be...love? Surely not!* She chided. *I hardly know the man.* Her eyes locked on his. *Yes, there was definitely something going on between them. But could it truly be love? How did one know?*

These are the thoughts that tumbled around in her head in the brief moment they stood gazing at each other, neither speaking a word for fear of ruining the moment.

"Catherine!"

The moment was ruined. It was Aunt Margaret. She came hurriedly out onto the patio and approached them, anger evident on her face.

"What do you think you are doing, young lady?" she nearly bellowed, "standing out here alone, in the darkness, with a strange man. You disgrace yourself, Catherine."

"But, Aunt Mar-"

"Do not even attempt an explanation, Catherine," said Aunt Margaret, holding up her hand to stave off any further comment. "It is quite plain, to anyone with eyes to see, that this is highly inappropriate behavior."

Shooing Catherine along, she continued her tirade. "I demand that you return to the ball immediately, and forget this meeting ever happened. And pray, no one else witnessed this indiscretion, or you will be ruined, girl. Now, go," she commanded.

Holding back tears, Catherine rushed away back into the ballroom.

Turning to face the young man, Lady Hathaway fixed him with a disdainful glare.

"And you, sir," she said with all the fierceness she could muster. "I don't know who you are, or what you game is, but I advise you to steer clear of my niece. She is an innocent who will not be spoiled by the likes of you." Looking down her nose at him, she added, "You will do well to heed my warning, young man. Catherine is, and will forever be, far above your station, and I have plans for a great marriage match for her. Plans that will not be altered," she added as she turned and huffed away.

Garrett stood frozen in shock, trying to make sense of what just happened. One moment he was having a lovely conversation with the most beautiful woman he'd ever seen. The next, he was being verbally assaulted without any idea why. Granted, he knew he had forgone propriety when he's approached the girl, but nothing untoward had happened. He'd been the perfect gentleman the entire time he and the lady had been talking. But the older woman, who appeared to be her aunt, had come at him with such venom, forbidding him to ever speak to the girl again. Now what was he to do? Of course, he had to see her again. He had a very strong feeling that things were just beginning for them. He would have to find a way.

The next day, Catherine asked for a breakfast tray to be brought up to her room. She was still angry and had no wish to see or to speak to her aunt. Tears came unbidden when she thought back on how her aunt had humiliated her in front of Mr. Brennen. Catherine knew their meeting like that had not been proper, but surely Aunt Margaret could see that nothing unseemly had occurred during their brief exchange.

Catherine had not spoken a word to her aunt since returning to the ballroom last night. She'd finished out the dances with little enthusiasm and a heavy heart. Whenever she tried to catch Garrett's eye, he seemed to be purposely avoiding her. By the time the ball had ended, and she and her aunt were headed home, she was in an extremely foul mood. She hardly responded to her aunt's attempts at conversation, finally leaning against the side of the carriage and feigning sleep in order to avoid conversation altogether.

Upon their arrival at home, Catherine roused herself, rushing inside and upstairs before her aunt had even had the chance to alight from the carriage. Though it had been in the wee hours of the morning when they'd returned, Catherine was unable to sleep. She had tossed and turned, alternating with pacing and crying, until dawn, when she'd finally grown tired enough to sleep for a few hours.

Catherine disliked being so angry, especially with her beloved aunt, but she was not yet ready to forgive. Aunt Margaret was being so unreasonable, forbidding her to have any further contact with Mr. Brennen. It wasn't as if Catherine was planning to marry him for goodness sake, though he did seem to be a very interesting gentleman, educated, and well-mannered. Catherine only wished to become better acquainted with him in the way of forming a sort of friendship. At least, that's what she kept telling herself, but she was not very convincing.

After she had eaten a bit of breakfast, Catherine grew drowsy. Lying back on her bed, she fell into a fitful sleep, where visions of amber eyes and luscious lips haunted her. After several hours, she awoke feeling only slightly rested. She asked her maid, Abby, to prepare a bath, hoping a long, warm soak would restore her and help lift her spirits.

Bathed and dressed and feeling at least a bit more refreshed, Catherine descended the stairs and headed toward the library. Perhaps a bit of reading would distract her from her sullen state and occupy her thoughts with something other than Mr. Garrett Brennen. She randomly pulled a book from a shelf and moved to sit in her favorite reading chair. She'd only read a few pages when sleep once again overtook her. This time, it was a deep and peaceful sleep.

She awakened with a start. There were voices in the hall. One of them was Aunt Margaret's. The other was a male voice. *Could it be?* She strained her ears, trying to find familiarity in the deep pitched voice. *Surely after the way her aunt treated him, he wouldn't dare show his face here. Who then?*

"Catherine, dear," she heard her aunt call out. "You have a visitor…a gentleman caller."

Eager to put an end to the suspense, Catherine quickly rose to her feet, straightening her gown and patting her hair in place. She walked down the hall toward the drawing room. Reaching the doorway, she paused. Her aunt sat in her favorite winged back chair near the fire. Across from her, on the tapestry covered couch, sat Lord Moreland. Upon seeing her, Harry immediately stood, grabbing the bouquet of flowers lying next to him on the couch.

"Miss Elmsworth, how good it is to see you," he said, bowing slightly. Remembering he held the flowers, he took a few steps forward, offering them to her.

"Lord Moreland." She nodded slightly as she took the proffered bouquet. "What brings you here?" Realizing the rudeness of her question, Catherine tried again. "Forgive my rudeness, my lord. It is just that I am surprised to see you out on a social call so early in the day after such a late evening of entertainment."

"Do sit down, both of you," said Lady Hathaway. "I've ordered tea to be brought in." As the young people moved to seat themselves, Aunt Margaret sent Catherine a pointed look, silently warning her to be polite.

"So, tell us, Lord Moreland," her aunt continued. "Did you enjoy the ball last night?"

"Oh yes, Lady Hathaway. I had a very pleasant time indeed," Harry replied. Glancing at Catherine, his cheeks coloring slightly, he added, "It was a pleasure to make the acquaintance of so many new people."

A maid appeared with the tea cart, halting conversation as she placed the tea tray on the table next to Aunt Margaret. Both Harry and Catherine sat uncomfortably quiet until Lady Hathaway had served the three of them their tea and biscuits.

As neither Catherine nor Harry seemed eager to further the conversation, Margaret continued prodding Harry with questions.

"You are recently down from university, are you not, Harry?"

"Yes, my lady, that is correct. I completed my studies this past June."

"And what were you studying? I mean to say, what particular course of study were you taking?"

"As you may be aware, Lady Hathaway, my father is a horse man. My family raises thoroughbreds, hunting horses. It is my desire to follow my father into the business of buying and selling fine horseflesh. To that end, I studied primarily mathematics and business." Glancing again at Catherine, he hoped to gain her favor by showing himself as an industrious and enterprising man, who would be able to provide well for his future family. She seemed uninterested in anything he had to say. "I am quite accomplished in both subjects," he added quietly, not wishing to seem overly boastful. He would leave the boasting to his friend, Arthur.

"I see," Lady Hathaway replied. "And you are Lord Mosbey's eldest son if I remember correctly."

"You remember correctly, my lady, in that I am also his only son." Harry would swear he heard a slight snicker come from Catherine's direction, but when he looked her way, she seemed to be examining the remains of her tea. She didn't even glance up. "I have two younger sisters, Lady Mary and Lady Anna," he added.

"Well, that seems a promising enterprise for you, then, and a large inheritance too, I would imagine. Any young woman should consider herself lucky to win your affection with the potential of a future agreement of marriage." She cast a sidelong glance at her niece.

Catherine could hold back no longer.

"Aunt Margaret, please," she bid in a raised tone. "Let the man be. Surely, he didn't come here to visit with the intention of being questioned about his future goals, or to be put on display as a worthy marriage prospect."

Harry gaped at her, astonished, in part due to the fact that she had spoken so earnestly in his defense, and also because he had, in fact, conjured this visit with at least some sort of intent of furthering his acquaintance with Miss Elmsworth in the hope that she might one day consider a marriage alliance with him.

Margaret harrumphed, straightening herself in her chair and squaring her shoulders. She looked pointedly at her niece.

"I was merely making conversation, Catherine, something you seem reluctant and unwilling to do."

Setting her teacup and saucer on the small table next to her, Catherine faced her aunt squarely.

"I am perfectly willing to participate in the conversation, Auntie, if we could perhaps find a more suitable topic to discuss, one of general interest that does not draw attention to one particular person in the room nor promote the agenda of another." She smiled sweetly at her aunt.

Turning to Harry, she asked, "Do you enjoy books, Lord Moreland?"

Harry, who had remained silent during the interchange between the two women, looked at her, still somewhat bewildered.

"I…." he faltered. "Yes, I suppose you could say I enjoy a book now and then." He smiled weakly at Catherine, certain she was finding him to be a dullard. "And you, Miss Elmsworth, do you enjoy them?"

"Most of the time, I find I enjoy the company of books more than the company of people," Catherine answered. Recognizing at once how her comment could be construed as rude, she added, "Present company accepted, of course."

"Thank you for saying so, my lady. The thought that you might enjoy the presence of my company, even a little, pleases me more than I can say," he answered, a light blush warming his checks.

"You are always more than welcome here, Lord Moreland," gushed Aunt Margaret. "We are honored to have such a distinguished young gentleman as our guest."

"Thank you, Lady Hathaway," Harry spoke as he stood, "and I thank you for the tea, but I fear I must take my leave as I have some errands to attend to on my father's behalf."

The ladies both stood as well. Taking Margaret's hand, he said, "Good day, Lady Hathaway." Turning to take Catherine's hand in his, and bowing slightly over it, he said his goodbyes and left through the drawing room door. Catherine turned to leave the room as well.

"One moment, please, Catherine," said her aunt. Catherine stopped but did not turn to face her. She remained quiet.

"Please sit, dear," said Margaret. "I have something I wish to say to you."

Catherine turned and haltingly made her way back to the couch, where she sat with her back straight and her hands in her lap. She still refused to speak.

"Despite what feelings you may have toward me at this time, I expect you to be courteous and treat all of our guests with respect."

Watching Catherine take in a deep breath, as if preparing to say something, Margaret held up her hand to stop any forthcoming comments.

"I am aware that Lord Moreland may not be your idea of a suitable husband, but he is a very intelligent, very good-looking, and a tolerably pleasant man, and his family is very well-to-do. I only mean to encourage you not to discard him by the wayside before he's even been given a chance at winning your affection."

There was still no response from Catherine.

"Have you anything to say to me, girl?"

Still refusing to look at her aunt, Catherine said, "It appears, Aunt Margaret, as if you have already made all of my decisions for me regarding whom I am to show favor to and whom I am never to speak to. What is there for me to say? Should I thank you for saving me the trouble of making my own choices regarding my future and whom I might want to find friendship with?"

She held back fresh tears as thoughts of Garrett once again found their place in her mind. And it wasn't just her mind that he occupied. Even after such a brief exchange that they'd shared, he had already found his way into her heart. She could not bear the thought of never seeing him again, of never speaking to him, of never touching him. Yes, she was ready to admit it was more, much more than mere friendship she wanted from Garrett Brennen.

"One day you will thank me, young lady," said her aunt, rising to go. "You will realize when you are happily married to a man of status and means who is able to give you everything you will ever need or want, that I was right in cutting that young violinist off before he could persuade you into some sort of debauchery that would bring you to your ruin." Reaching the door, she paused. "You heed my words, Catherine," she said as she left the room.

The Earl's Masquerade

CHAPTER FOUR

"If life for me hath joy or light,
'Tis all from thee,
My thoughts by day, my dreams by night
Are but of thee, of only thee."
from *'Tis All For Thee*

Eventually things were smoothed over between Catherine and her aunt. Catherine found it impossible to harbor anger against her beloved aunt for very long. After all, Aunt Margaret had done so much for her, she owed the lady a great deal for all the generosity and love she had been given over the years. She could never repay her aunt, in any way, other than to be the best pseudo daughter she could be, and that meant obeying her aunt even when she wasn't so inclined.

A few weeks had passed, with Catherine and Margaret attending several small parties and social events. At each one of them, Catherine could not keep her eyes from searching the rooms for a particular young man, but he was never seen. She tried to be on her best behavior in spite of it, and once or twice, even found that she was indeed enjoying herself and the company of the new friends she had met.

Several of the young men, including Lord Moreland and both of his friends, Mr. Worth and Mr. Fellows, had called on Catherine, but she had not given any of them any encouragement toward a relationship other than that of friendship. She particularly enjoyed spending her time with Harry and his younger sister, Mary, who was the same age as Catherine. The three of them were often seen together enjoying one another's company.

Mary and Catherine had found they had much in common, especially a love of reading. They spent many hours together in Aunt Margaret's library, reading, discussing books they had read, and generally delighting in their mutual love of books. They would spend a whole afternoon extolling the virtues of their favorite fictional heroes, as well as the more appealing qualities of some of the men they were acquainted with.

Mary was particularly fond of blondes like herself, and men who had a bit of a playful nature but were kindhearted.

"I would prefer a man who was English, or maybe Scottish," Mary proclaimed one afternoon as they sat daydreaming of romance. "Or French…the French are very intriguing. What is your preference, Catherine?"

Thinking of one man in particular, Catherine gazed leisurely out the window. "I think I prefer an Irishman," she answered dreamily, "one with wild dark hair and amber eyes."

Mary quirked a brow as she turned to Catherine, "Why Irish? The Irish seem so common, not nearly as interesting as a Scottish highlander or a French aristocrat. Are not the Irish mainly farmers?"

Catherine was a bit offended by Mary's high-brow tone. "I'm sure there are commoners in Ireland, just as there are here in England, but there are also wealthy landed gentry and aristocrats as well." She frowned, adding, "I think you may judge others too harshly, Mary, especially those you have no personal knowledge of or acquaintance with. There are good and bad at every class level. People shouldn't be judged solely on their social standing or how much money they have."

Catherine continued her rant as Mary gaped at her in astonishment. "What I mean to say is, a person's worth should not be based only on the amount of money they have. It should be taken into account their moral character, their personal integrity, their generosity toward those less fortunate, and many other things besides their wealth or which class they happened to be born into."

Mary considered what Catherine said. "Perhaps much of what you say is true, Catherine. Certainly, being born into wealth and upper class does not guarantee a person to be of good character. Still, the rules of society are put into place for a reason. If everyone were to go around interacting with one another without rules, the result would be mayhem. Imagine if you and I were to engage in social activities with the working-class townies. People on either side wouldn't know what to make of it. It would cause chaos and scandal. Of course, people of all social standings should be treated politely and with dignity, but I believe we should stick to our own in terms of social engagement."

"You may be right, Mary," Catherine acquiesced. "Still, I can't agree that, should the heart choose to attach itself to one of a different circumstance, one could just ignore it under the guise of propriety and turn away from it. Surely, the heart knows when it finds true love wherever that may be."

Mary stared back at her friend, eyes wide in astonishment. "I believe there is much more to relationships, other than what one *feels*," she said with a bit of a haughty air about her. "Surely, finding someone who can provide for you in a manner of which you are accustomed is of some importance when choosing a partner."

"I suppose you know more about such things than I do," Catherine sighed. "It just seems to me such a sterile way of pursuing friendships and romantic relationships. I think that I should prefer to marry for love above all else, for I believe that if you truly love, then you should be able to withstand all of life's circumstances that may come your way."

"That is a fairy tale way of thinking, Catherine," her friend chastised. "I believe you have read too many of your beloved novels, my friend."

"Perhaps," Catherine agreed, "but I would still like to believe that true love is a real possibility, and that one shouldn't have to settle for less.

On one of their afternoons together, the two friends had decided that a visit to the book shop in town was in order. Calling for the carriage to be brought round, they bid Aunt Margaret farewell and headed off to town.

Browsing the shelves for a new book to buy, Catherine was startled when she nearly bumped into someone in the poetry section. Gasping in surprise, she looked up and straight into those familiar fawn-colored eyes. They enveloped her, and she found herself momentarily frozen, unable to move or speak.

"Garrett," she whispered, finally finding a little of her voice. Clearing her throat, she corrected herself. "Mr. Brennen."

"We meet again, Miss Elmsworth," he said, smiling down at her. There were the dimples. She found that she was very fond of those dimples. "It seems we keep bumping in to one another," he said, grinning.

"Yes," she said meekly, bowing her head as she cursed her heated cheeks. Focusing, and finally finding her voice, she asked, "Are you shopping for something in particular, Mr. Brennen?"

"*Catherine.*" Her name sounded wonderful spoken from his lips. "I know we are newly acquainted, but I feel as if I have known you a very long time. Whenever it is just the two of us, I would prefer for you to call me Garrett."

"Y-yes," she stammered. "*Garrett,*" she replied. Spying the small volume he held in his hand, she nodded toward it asking, "Have you made your selection, then?"

Turning the small book in his hand so that she could read the cover, he replied, "A collection of Thomas Moore's poetry. Have you read any of his works?"

"Oh yes," said Catherine. "He is one of my favorite poets. He writes the most beautiful love poems," she added. She felt the blasted color rise in her cheeks again at the mere mention of love poetry. *What a thing to be discussing,* she thought, *especially with this man.*

Noting the bright coloration of Catherine's cheeks, Garrett grinned, pressing her further. "And do you have a favorite poem?" he asked leaning just a wee bit closer to her.

Meeting his eyes, Catherine began to quote from memory her favorite passage from Moore's *M.P; Or The Blue-Stocking.*

"To keep one sacred flame,
  Through life unchilled, unmoved,
To love in wintry age the same
  As first in youth we loved;
To feel that we adore
  To such refined excess,
That though the heart would break with more,
  We could not live with less;"

Holding her gaze, Garrett joined her on the last phrase.

"This is love, faithful love,
    Such as saints might feel above."

As they finished the poem, Garrett was just inches from her. Catherine could feel his warm breath on her cheek. Looking up into his copper eyes, she was again mesmerized by them. Neither of them moved for what seemed an eternity as they gazed at each other. Catherine, sure that Garrett was about to kiss her, startled at her friend's voice.

"Catherine, did you...find...anything?" Mary asked, coming around the corner. Garrett and Catherine quickly drew apart, but not before Mary was able to take in the scene before her. "Well," she smiled, knowingly, "It appears you *did* find something."

"Mary," said Catherine, flustered. "Allow me to introduce you to Mr. Garrett Brennen." She weakly gestured toward Garrett. Unable to meet either of their gazes, she continued, "Mr. Brennen, may I introduce my friend, Lady Mary Fatham."

"Lady Mary," said Garrett, bowing graciously. "It is my great honor to meet a friend of Miss Elmsworth's."

Realizing that this man might be thwarting her brother's chances to win Catherine, Mary decided to play the part of devoted sister and champion Harry.

"Perhaps you also know my brother, Lord Moreland, Mr. Brennen," she said quite innocently. "He is also a very close friend of Catherine's. In fact, I expect he will make a claim on her affections very soon." She smiled sweetly at Garrett.

Casting a quizzical glance at Catherine, Garrett replied, "No, I'm afraid I haven't had the pleasure of meeting your brother, my lady. However, I am certain that any friend of Catherine's would be a worthy acquaintance." Garrett smiled back at her just as sweetly.

"As the eldest son of my father, The Earl of Mosbey, my brother stands to inherit quite a large sum," Mary said smugly. "He would certainly be quite the catch for any woman who held his affection." Turning to Catherine, she said, "Shall we go, Catherine?"

Shaken at her friend's declaration, Catherine said, "Yes." She glanced up at Garrett, unable to decipher what she saw in his eyes. "Yes, we should probably be going," she offered lamely.

Garrett laid the small book he held back on the shelf. "Well then, ladies, if you will excuse me, I will also be taking my leave. Lady Mary." He nodded toward Mary. "Miss Elmsworth," he said, turning to Catherine. In a barely audible whisper meant for her ears alone, he added, "A great pleasure as always." With that, he turned and was gone.

"Well, *that* was certainly a surprise to come upon," said Mary. "Whatever could you possibly be thinking Catherine, allowing that man to stand in such close proximity to you? My word, it seemed almost as if he were going to kiss you!"

Yes, it did seem so, didn't it? Catherine mused, smiling to herself. Ignoring Mary's outburst, she retrieved the small volume from the shelf in order to purchase it. Turning to her friend, she said, "Shall we go, Mary?"

After setting Mary down at the Fatham residence along the way, Catherine arrived back home emotionally exhausted, both from her unexpected meeting with Garrett, and from

Mary's constant harassment for the duration of the ride home. She chided Catherine non-stop for her foolishness and impropriety at the book shop. For her part, Catherine remained quiet during the ride, unresponsive to her friend's chastisement. Her thoughts had all been absorbed by a particular man, one with copper eyes.

Aunt Margaret had decided that she and Catherine would be having a dinner party. There were to be a dozen people in attendance, including Catherine and Margaret themselves. The invited guests included Lord Moreland, his mother and father, Lord and Lady Mosbey, and his sisters, Lady Mary and Lady Anna. Also on the guest list, was Lord Harington, whom Catherine had not encountered since the ball where they had first been introduced.

Catherine chose a golden yellow gown trimmed with brown, almost copper colored lace, for the party. She had chosen it purposely, knowing that Aunt Margaret had planned this party in an attempt to distract her niece's thoughts from Garrett, and the coppery trim was a reminder of the eyes, and the man, Catherine did not want to be distracted from. In fact, she had been spending a good portion of her days in the garden with her small book of poetry at hand. Over and over, she read the poem she and Garrett had shared. With each reading came a fresh longing to see him again.

There were voices coming from the drawing room as Catherine descended the stairs. It sounded as if most of the guests had arrived. Catherine made her way to the room, pasting a strained smile on her face that she hoped would be convincing enough for both Aunt Margaret and their guests. It was destined to be a long evening.

Lady Hathaway stood near the fireplace conversing with Lady Mosbey and the parson's wife, Mrs. Grant. Harry stood with his father and the vicar, Mr. Nathaniel Grant. Seeing Catherine enter the room, his eyes gleamed as he smiled at her with a slight nod. His sisters, seated on the couch, were immersed in animated conversation. Three men were gathered near the corner of the room and appeared to be in deep discussion. The two men whom she could see were Harry's friends, Mr. Worth and Mr. Fellows. The other gentleman, whom she viewed from the back, Catherine determined to be Lord Harington.

Spying her niece, Lady Hathaway burst forth, exclaiming, "Ah, here is my lovely niece, now!" Taking Catherine's arm, she drew her further into the room. "Ladies," she said to the two women she had been in conversation with, "You will remember my niece, Catherine, from the ball last month. Catherine, you remember Lady Mosbey, I'm sure, and Mrs. Grant, the vicar's wife."

Catherine greeted each of the ladies before her aunt twirled around to the group. "Ladies and Gentlemen, shall we retreat to the dining room?"

Husbands returned to wives to escort them into the dining room. Harry, being closest to where Catherine stood, rushed over to her and, offering his arm, said, "Catherine, may I have the pleasure of escorting you to dinner?"

"Certainly, Harry," she answered casually, as they had become fairly close aquaintances in the past months. Catherine smiled up at him as she placed her hand on his arm. Lord Mosbey and Vicar Grant escorted their wives, Arthur and James each escorted one of Harry's sisters, and Lord Harington escorted Lady Hathaway to table.

As the guests all seated themselves in the dining room, Catherine was pleased to find that James was seated next to her. She had hoped she would not be forced to endure Mr. Fellow's braggadocio for the entire meal. Luckily, he had been seated at the far end of the table with the vicar and his wife. Mr. Grant should be able to keep Arthur's boasting to a minimum. Lord

Harington, Mary and Anna were seated across the table from Catherine, Harry, and James.

"Have you been to any more balls, Miss Elmsworth?" James asked once dinner was underway.

"No, I'm afraid not," Catherine replied. "However, I believe Lord and Lady Mosbey are hosting one next week, is that not true, Harry?" she asked, turning toward Harry.

"Yes, they are, Catherine, and James, of course you are invited if you will still be in town then," he added.

Turning to James, Catherine asked, "Are you going on a trip, Mr. Worth?" Catherine noticed Anna's close attention to their conversation from across the table.

"I am to leave Thursday next, so I am afraid I will not be able to attend the ball, Harry, though I do sorely hate to miss it," he said, casting a quick glance at Anna. To Catherine, he said, "I am going to visit my family in Yorkshire. My sister is to be married."

"Oh, how lovely," replied Catherine. "A wedding is always such a lovely occasion."

Sensing some anxiousness from across the table, Catherine asked, "And how long will you be staying up north?"

Witnessing yet another glance in Anna's direction, Catherine became intrigued. It seemed to her as if James were not having this conversation with her at all, but instead, was directing his replies to the young blonde across the table. They were being very subtle about it, but there was a definite...something...going on between them that one would only notice if one was paying close attention, which Catherine was. She made a mental note to speak to Anna about it later.

Drawing her attention away from Anna, Catherine caught Lord Harington watching her. As their eyes met, he nodded very slightly and offered her a brief smile before turning his attention to his dinner. *He is a strange one*, thought Catherine. As yet, he hadn't spoken a word to her this evening, but Catherine continued to feel his eyes on her as the meal progressed. She could not decide if it pleased her or annoyed her.

Later, when the ladies returned to the drawing room, having left the men to their after-dinner port, Catherine was able to get Anna alone for a moment.

"Anna, please tell me if I am being too intrusive, but I am quite curious. Do I sense an attraction between you and Mr. Worth?"

Poor Anna's cheeks turned bright pink at the mere mention of James. "Oh dear!" she exclaimed. "Is it obvious?"

"Perhaps not to the casual observer, but I did become aware of some non-verbal exchanges between the two of you at dinner." As gently as she could, so as not to worry Anna further, she asked, "Has James been courting you, Anna?"

"Oh, no!" Anna replied adamantly. "Mother and Father say I am too young to be courted. I have not yet had my coming out season. They say I must wait another year until I am sixteen years of age."

"But you are interested in James?" Catherine persisted.

"Yes," Anna confessed. "I have always had an attraction to my brother's friend."

"And by my observations, the feelings are mutual. Have the two of you discussed it?"

"Not in a serious manner, no, but once when James was visiting, my father asked him if there was any particular young lady he was interested in courting. James replied that he was waiting for one of my father's daughters to grow up. And there have been a few other similar but vague comments."

Anna grew more flustered. "Perhaps I am altogether wrong in my assumptions, but I truly do believe he feels the same way I do."

"I am sure you assume correctly, Anna. James is probably just abiding by your parents' wishes and waiting until you are of age to make his feelings known."

A hopeful look came to Anna's features. "Oh, I hope you are right, Catherine. I cannot imagine feeling the way I do about anyone besides James."

At that moment the men re-joined the ladies. As they entered, the young men congregated around Catherine, vying for her attention. Except for Lord Harington, who stood off to the side, unsmiling, observing their flirtatious overtures.

The Earl's Masquerade

CHAPTER FIVE

"If I speak to thee in Friendship's name,
Thou think'st I speak too coldly;
If I mention Love's devoted flame,
Thou say'st I speak too boldly.
Between these two unequal fires,
Why doom me thus to hover?
I'm a friend, if such thy heart requires,
If more thou seek'st, a lover.
Which shall it be? How shall I woo?
Fair one, choose between the two."
from *How Shall I Woo?*

Catherine was surprised the following day when there was a knock at the door, and Lord Harington appeared.

"Pardon me for such a short notice, Miss Elmsworth, but I thought perhaps you might be willing to accompany me on a ride through the park." He paused, noting her surprise. Looking perhaps a bit less sure of himself, he went on. "Your aunt assured me last night that you would welcome the outing on such a fine day as this."

If she were to have put any thought into the matter, she would have guessed that he, of all the eligible young males attending last night's dinner, had shown the least amount of interest in her. Yet, here he was at her door, apparently with an aim at courting her.

Aunt Margaret, needless to say, was ecstatic over the idea and couldn't usher Catherine out of the door fast enough. No wonder she had been so adamant this morning that Catherine should wear one of her new day dresses. It was apparent that she had been doing some plotting without Catherine's knowledge.

Catherine couldn't deny that she was pleased with the attention. Lord Harington was an extremely handsome man and many a young woman would swoon at just the thought of a carriage ride alone with him. Of course, they would not be entirely alone, as two coachmen would be with them. Still, there would be a certain privacy afforded them within the confines of the carriage. Catherine wasn't so sure she was ready for this. However, it would be rude of her not to accept at this point, so she agreed to the ride.

She turned to summon Abby to ask her to fetch her shawl, only to discover her already there with shawl and bonnet in hand. *Aunt Margaret wasted no time, did she?* Catherine said to herself with a smile. Abby helped Catherine on with both her hat and her shawl. As Lord Harington stepped aside, allowing her to exit the doorway,

Catherine saw that the top of his carriage was down, and she was immediately thankful that the hat she wore had a bit of a wider brim that would offer some protection from the sun.

Once the two of them were seated comfortably inside, Lord Harington directed the driver to proceed to Hyde Park. Aunt Margaret stood on the stoop waving them off. As they pulled away from the house, Catherine felt suddenly nervous and could not think of a single thing to say. They sat facing each other in silence. She could feel the earl's eyes on her. She looked over to find him staring at her.

"It appears your aunt did not inform you that I would be paying a visit today. Please forgive me for the imposition, Miss Elmsworth. It is kind of you to accept my invitation without prior notice." When Catherine said nothing, he continued. "You could have said no," he offered with a tiny quirk of his lips.

Meeting his gaze, Catherine said, "As you well know, my lord, it would have been highly improper, not to mention very rude, had I declined."

"I would have understood."

There was another lull in conversation.

With a heavy sigh, Catherine said, "As long as we are to spend some time together, and since you are well known to my aunt, you may as well call me Catherine, at least when we are in private company."

"A beautiful name for a beautiful lady," Harington replied, his voice a fraction deeper, and his eyes never leaving her face. "Thank you, Catherine, and I must insist, when we are alone, that you call me Brooks."

Settling back into her seat, she peered at him. "Brooks," she said. "That is an interesting name. I don't believe I have ever heard it before. Is it a family name?"

"No," Brooks answered. "It is actually a mistake." He smiled at her confused look before continuing. "My mother was keenly interested in the name Brooke for her firstborn, whether it be male or female, so when the time came that she had a son, she named him…me…Brooke. However, in the notation of the record of my birth, the name was somehow written down as Brooks with an 's' in place of the 'e'." He shrugged slightly. "Rather than have it changed, my mother decided she rather fancied the name Brooks and left it at that."

"I believe it suits you, my lord. An unusual name for an unusual man," Catherine replied, smiling.

"Do you see me as unusual, Catherine?" Brooks asked.

"Somewhat so, yes," she answered, narrowing her eyes as she examined him. "You are not like the other young men I have encountered," she continued. "You are more subdued, more observing." Pausing, she tilted her head slightly to one side, thinking, "And less exuberant," she added.

Brooks let out a laugh. "You make me sound quite the bore."

"No, no!" Catherine exclaimed. "That is not what I meant at all. Forgive me. It is just that you seem much more mature than most of the men I have met, more settled and more sure of yourself."

"Perhaps that is partly true," said Brooks. "As the eldest son, I had to take on much responsibility at a fairly young age, when my father died. I was barely nineteen when he was killed as the result of a hunting accident."

"I am so sorry, Brooks. I wasn't aware of your loss," Catherine said with all sincerity.

"It was some time ago," Brooks said. "He and some friends were part of a hunting party. They were deep in the woods when his horse became suddenly spooked by something, rearing up and throwing my father to the ground. He would have survived with a few bruises had his head not landed on a large rock jutting out of the ground. They said he died instantly and did not suffer. I like to believe that."

Catherine sat quietly, tears brimming her eyes.

"I am aware, my lady, that you, too, have suffered great loss," he said softly.

Barely nodding her head, she felt a single tear slide down her cheek. Brooks reached across to her and wiped it away with his thumb. Though his thumb barely touched her skin, Catherine felt the heat from his touch, as well as the coolness of the air against her cheek when Brooks drew his hand away.

No further words were spoken on the subject, but it felt to Catherine that some sort of bond had been created between them. They remained comfortably quiet in each other's company for several minutes.

"I believe we are coming upon some acquaintances of yours, Miss Elmsworth."

Brooks pointed just down the path in front of them. "Shall we stop and say how do you do?"

Turning in her seat, Catherine saw that he was referring to Harry, Arthur, and James, who were standing in a group near the edge of the path, engaged in conversation with several young women.

Though she had little desire to see or speak to them, she answered, "I suppose it would be very rude of us to pretend we haven't seen them."

"Very well, then, we will stop but a moment...unless you would like to stay longer," he suggested, a bit apprehensively.

"No, not at all," said Catherine. "Let's just stop for a few moments, just to be cordial, then we can be on our way."

Brooks signaled for the driver to stop near the group as they approached. James was the first to see them, waving and shouting out a greeting. Catherine and Brooks waved back. When the carriage halted, James hurried over to greet them.

Catherine looked over at Harry, just as he saw her and realized who she was with. His face grew suddenly sullen. Frowning, he approached the carriage. Arthur remained behind with the ladies.

"Lord Harington," said James, extending his hand to Brooks. "Miss Elmsworth," he turned to her with a warm smile. "So nice to see you out and about on such a fine day," he said.

"It is wonderful to see you, too, Mr. Worth. I hope you fellows are not getting up to any mischief out here today," she teased, just as Harry came up beside them. He looked angry.

"It appears we are not the ones seeking mischief, Catherine." He sounded angry as well. Catherine could not fathom why. She ignored his comment.

"Harry, so good to see you," she said. Addressing them both, she added, "I do hope that you both enjoyed the dinner party last night. Aunt Margaret was quite the hostess, was she not?"

"I had a wonderful time," James replied. "Everything was superb, including the company of three lovely young ladies," he teased. "I trust you enjoyed it as well, my lord." He turned to Brooks.

"Indeed. It was a lovely evening spent in lovely company," Brooks agreed. Harry appeared to be silently fuming. *Whatever is wrong with him?* Catherine wondered.

Glancing over at Catherine, Brooks said, "I am afraid, gentlemen, we must be on our way. I don't want to keep Miss Elmswoth out too long as the day grows warm." Tipping his hat to the men, he gave the order to the driver to continue on. Arthur called out to them and waved as they passed by. In a more subdued greeting, Brooks tipped his hat and Catherine gave a small nod.

"Mr. Worth seems a friendly sort," Brooks ventured in an attempt to re-start the conversation flowing.

"Yes, James is quite friendly," said Catherine. "I find he is of a much more pleasing nature than Mr. Fellows," she added before realizing what she was saying. She put her hand over her mouth, frowning. It was certainly bad manners to speak of someone thus, especially when conversing with a virtual stranger. *Why did she feel such a need to speak all of her thoughts to this man without the slightest censure?* Her eyes bulged in surprise at her lack of discretion. She looked at Lord Harington, who appeared to be holding back a smile, though his eyes danced with mirth.

"Do not worry, Catherine, you may speak candidly with me." Serious again, Brooks looked at her intently. "I will never betray your trust by repeating anything told to me in confidence or within a private conversation between the two of us." Smiling once more, he added, "And anyway, I am quite in agreement with you on that matter. In all my previous encounters with him, Lord Fellows has appeared to be highly enamored of himself, as he himself is often the subject of most of his conversations."

Suppressing a giggle, Catherine asked, "So, you know Henry, James, and Arthur?"

"I am of some familiarity with them. I have encountered them at White's on a few occasions, though I don't often frequent the establishment."

Her brow furrowed, Catherine tried to ascertain what might have been troubling Harry. "Did Lord Moreland seem a bit off to you?" she asked Brooks. "I could have sworn he seemed angry over something, though he barely said a word. Maybe it is just my imagining things."

Brooks gazed at Catherine, a look of amusement once again lighting up his face. "Surely, you are aware, Catherine, that Lord Moreland has set his eye on you with the strong intent of courting you. I am certain his anger was directed at me for the mere fact that I have taken you out for a ride in my carriage."

Catherine was shocked by his words, and somewhat embarrassed as well. "I am sure you are quite mistaken, my lord," she said, unable to meet his eyes. "Harry and I are friends, nothing more," she declared with finality.

"Perhaps then, dear lady, it would be wise for you to make him aware of that fact, if it is indeed the case."

"Of course it is!" Catherine insisted. "And Harry must know it. I have never given him any indication that we were anything otherwise."

"I am certain you believe what you say to be true, but I can assure you, that man has other ideas in his head."

Tilting up her chin and narrowing her eyes at him, Catherine asked, "And what makes you so certain of his intentions, my lord?"

Leaning forward in his seat, his gaze fixed on Catherine, Brooks took her hand gently in his. "I am certain, Miss Elmsworth, because my intentions are the same as his," he spoke in a deep throaty voice. Lowering his lips, he kissed the back of Catherine's hand ever so lightly, his eyes never leaving hers.

A small gasp escaped Catherine as Brooks released her hand back onto her lap. Though she wanted to reprimand him for taking such liberties, no words came to her. In spite of herself, she had to admit it had felt rather nice, his lips touching her skin. She felt the heat travel up her neck and into her cheeks. *Blast it!* she thought. *Why must my feverish cheeks always betray me?* Pulling her fan out from her reticule, she began fanning herself with urgency, making some rubbish reference to the heat. She had no idea what she was saying. Her mind was a jumble of thoughts, and not one of them could be made to form into anything coherent.

Thankfully, Brooks remained silent for the duration of the ride. He appeared to be lost in his own thoughts, for which Catherine was most grateful. It afforded her the opportunity to gather her own wayward thoughts and dizzy emotions into some form of cohesion.

The carriage came to an abrupt halt, and Catherine looked up to find they had arrived back at her aunt's house. Much relieved, she could hardly wait to remove herself from the carriage and from the presence of Lord Harington. The ease she had felt so briefly with him was now gone and she felt as uncomfortable as when the ride first began.

Stepping out of the carriage, Brooks turned and offered his hand to help Catherine out. The very last thing she wanted to do right now was touch him again, but she had no choice. Slipping her hand into his, she removed herself from the carriage as quickly as she could.

Turning to face him as she took her hand from his, Catherine forced herself to look him in the eye. "Thank you, Lord Harington, for a lovely ride," she said, as she turned toward the house. "Good day to you."

"Perhaps we may do it again soon," he called after her. She refused to answer or even look back at him as the door opened in front of her and she rushed inside.

Closing the door behind her, Weston, the butler, asked, "Are you all right, Miss Elmsworth?" Catherine heard real concern in his voice as he hovered about her anxiously. "Are you unwell?" He straightened suddenly. "Lord Harington did not harm you, did he?" he queried, looking for all the world as if he were ready to go out and clobber a man half his age if there had been any wrongdoing upon her person.

Catherine had to smile at the fervency of his inquiry. It was sweet of him to endeavor to defend her honor, even against a man like Harington. She quickly put his worry to rest.

"No harm has come to me, Weston. I am fine," she claimed. "Perhaps just a bit overheated, and in need of some refreshment," she offered, hoping to assuage his concern. "Would you please fetch me a cool drink, Weston, and bring it into the drawing room?"

"Right away, my lady," Weston replied, bowing. Righting himself, he left to retrieve her drink as Catherine made her way down the hall and into the drawing room.

Oh bother! There sat Aunt Margaret in her favorite chair, a look of curious anticipation on her face. Catherine couldn't very well reverse her steps and flee at this point, so she continued on into the room, hoping her color had returned to normal. She forced her breathing to a slower pace as she sat on the couch across from her aunt.

Aunt Margaret seemed to be about to burst. "Catherine!" she exclaimed, feigning surprise. "Back so soon from your ride?" she inquired. Not waiting for a reply, she continued. "And how did you find Lord Harington, my dear? Did you enjoy his company?"

Smiling at her aunt's bombardment of questions, Catherine replied, "Please, slow down, Aunt Margaret. I only just walked in the door."

Weston came in with a glass of cold lemonade on a tray which he offered to Catherine. After taking a rather long drink of the cool beverage, Catherine settled back comfortably on the couch and turned her attention to her aunt.

"Lord Harington was a gentleman, very attentive, and a good conversationalist," she declared, hoping to satisfy her aunt's probing. "I found him to be quite amiable, and, yes, I did enjoy his company well enough." *Right up until that last bit,* she thought. She pushed the thought out of her mind, lest she give herself away to her aunt. Aunt Margaret was nothing if not observant. It would not due at all to have her see Catherine flustered. She would likely read much more into it than there actually was. There really wasn't anything at all to read into. *Was there?*

Aunt Margaret sat on the edge of her seat, waiting for Catherine to elaborate on her outing with Lord Harington. She was positive it would only escalate her aunt's matchmaking attempts were she to inform her of the earl's proposed intentions. *And what of Harry?* She wondered. *Could what Lord Harington had said be true? Did Harry wish to court her?* Catherine hoped not.

All this matchmaking and courtship nonsense was beginning to try her nerves. She did not wish to be courted by anyone, unless he was a beautiful violinist with long, dark hair, brown eyes, and a delightfully dimpled smile. Catherine felt she had already lost her heart to just such a man, and no one else would suit her.

"What is it, dear?" Aunt Margaret asked, leaning forward in her chair with a worried look.

Oh dear! thought Catherine. *Now I've done it.* "Whatever do you mean, Auntie?" she asked as innocently as possible.

Her aunt was not fooled for one minute. "It's just that you were frowning, love. I thought there must be something you have neglected to tell me. I hope nothing untoward happened while you were out and about."

"No," answered Catherine. "In fact, nothing much happened at all." *There, maybe that would convince her aunt that she was wasting her time trying to make a match for her with Lord Harington.* "We did see Harry and his friends, Mr. Worth and Mr. Fellows, in the park. We stopped for a few moments to speak with them. Other than that, the afternoon was quite uneventful."

Before her aunt could pry further, Catherine stood. "If you will excuse me, Aunt Margaret, I believe I will go and change out of my dress and freshen up a bit." Without waiting for an answer, she left the room and hurried upstairs to her room.

Lying on her bed, Catherine let her thoughts drift and it was only a moment before they turned to Garrett. She wondered if she would ever see him again. He had not been at the latest parties she and her aunt had attended. They had been smaller, more intimate gatherings, but still she had hoped to see him. Maybe she could make another trip to the book shop in town with the possibility of seeing him there.

If only she knew more about him, maybe then she could somehow arrange to be in the places where he would be and just happen to run into him. She smiled at the thought of literally running into him, just as he had done that first night. To think that if she had arrived just a moment sooner or later, they might never have even met. She knew it was meant to be...*they* were meant to be. No matter what anyone else said or thought of it. It mattered little to her what the *ton* thought.

Of course, she did not desire to bring shame upon her aunt either. But what could she do? One cannot choose where the heart falls. And surely, she had truly fallen for Garrett. Though she hardly knew him, she knew there was something strong between them. She knew with a deep certainty he had felt it too.

How she wished her mother were here for her to talk to. Aunt Margaret was wonderful and had been so kind and generous to Catherine, and Catherine loved her aunt very much, but there were some things a girl just needed her mother for. For Catherine, this was one of them. She felt sure her mother would tell her to follow her heart. After all, that is what she herself had done, despite her family's protests, and she and Catherine's father had been wondrously in love since the moment they met. Perhaps that is what fueled Catherine's dreams that the same thing could be happening to her. Whatever was happening, Catherine knew she had to see Garrett again.

CHAPTER SIX

"Though, brimmed with blisses,
pure and rare,
Life's cup before me lay,
Unless thy love were mingled there
I'd spurn the draught away."
from *Oh! Yes, So Well*

Catherine and Lady Hathaway would be dining at the home of Lord and Lady Hawthorne. Though she had had opportunities to acquaint herself with them at various gatherings, Catherine had not visited the home of The Marquess and Marchioness since the night of their ball. The night she had first met Garrett. It was to be a small dinner party with only a dozen or so guests. Aunt Margaret had been quick to tell Catherine that Lord Harington would also be there.

Catherine sighed as she sat before her dressing table while Abby styled her hair.

"Are you not looking forward to the evening, my lady?" Abby asked, as she pinned up a few more auburn curls.

Catherine frowned a bit, though she tried not to. "I grow weary of all these parties, Abby. So much social engagement with others wears me out, both mentally and physically. I am not a social person by nature."

"I am well aware of that, my lady." Abby smiled at her mistress's reflection in the mirror. "We all here know how much you prefer the company of your books to the company of people."

That brought a smile to Catherine's face. "That is for certain, Abby. I do find the books more pleasant and undemanding than I do *most* people. In fact, I find that they also quite enjoy the silence that I prefer," she added with a sly smile. She and Abby laughed over her jest as Abby put the finishing touches on her hair.

Catherine had decided to wear her emerald dress, hoping that it would help lift her spirits. It was her favorite dress and she had been hoping to have a perfect opportunity to wear it. Tonight seemed as good a time as any, and she needed something to lighten her mood. She had been spending all her free time, and if she were honest about it, most of her busy time as well, thinking about Garrett, missing him. She longed to see him again, and she feared she never would.

From the time she and her aunt had arrived at Lord and Lady Hawthorne's, Catherine had done her very best to avoid Lord Harington, doing so in such a way as to not seem too obvious about it. She actively engaged in conversations with the other female guests, conversations which, at any other time, she would have found to be trite and boring, to say the least. How they could go on about the latest fashions, or who was seeing whom and other such gossip. Catherine could barely tolerate such mindless talk.

When the time came to enter the dining room, unfortunately, Lord Harington was quick to Catherine's side to escort her in, thereby guaranteeing for himself a seat next to her. Catherine turned away from him and immediately began speaking to the gentleman to her right. He was an older gentleman and seemed quite delighted that such a lovely young lady should show such an interest in conversing with him. Catherine managed to make it through most of the meal without speaking to Lord Harington.

However, near the end of the meal, he discreetly leaned into her side and whispered in her ear, "You can't avoid me forever, Catherine," just as she reached for her wine glass. His warm breath on her neck startled her and she lost her grasp on the glass, splashing wine over the table and her dress. Catherine sprang up out of her seat with a gasp.

Lord Harington also stood, grabbing his napkin and offering it to her. Catherine glared at him as she grasped the napkin he offered. His eyes begged her forgiveness. "I am so sorry, Catherine," he spoke quietly, unaware he had slipped into the familiar, and not wishing to draw further attention to them. Holding back tears of anger, Catherine said, "Please excuse me," to the other dinner guests and rushed out of the room. Lady Hawthorne ordered one of the maids to go along to attend to her.

Catherine was in tears when the maid servant arrived with a basin of water and some towels.

"There, there," said the maid, "not to worry, my lady. We'll take care of this." She began dabbing at the wet spot on the front of Catherine's gown. "You'll be good as new in no time at all. Now, stand over here near the fire, Miss Elmsworth, and your dress will dry in just a bit," she said, gently guiding Catherine over near the fireplace"

As Catherine sat waiting for her dress to dry, her tears subsided, anger taking their place.

How dare he! She thought. *Who does Lord Harington think he is?* She recalled his breath on her skin as he whispered the words in her ear, 'You can't avoid me forever, Catherine.' *Of all the nerve. He has no right to speak to me so intimately,* she silently fumed. *I have given him no indication that we are to be anything other than mere acquaintances.* And now her favorite dress was likely ruined. She was so angry at him. And hot. Yes, it was too hot sitting by the fire. She needed some fresh air.

As she walked down the hallway in search of a way to the back garden, Catherine heard music. She paused to listen, realizing suddenly that it was the music of a single sorrowful violin. Straining her ears, she tried to determine where it was coming from. Following the sound, she soon found her way to the french doors leading out to the back of the house. The music grew louder.

Pausing at the open doors, Catherine's breath caught when she saw the man standing at the far end of the terrace, facing away from her. He wore black form-fitting breeches, a white, long-sleeved, muslin shirt and a maroon waistcoat. He apparently had removed his tailcoat in order to afford him more freedom of movement as he played. It lay discarded on a stone bench nearby. He stood in a relaxed manner, completely engrossed in the music he was playing.

Catherine knew it was Garrett even before she saw the queue of brown locks tied at the nape of his neck with a black ribbon. She held her breath as she watched him play, thinking to herself that she had never seen nor heard anything so beautiful in all her life.

As he finished the tune, Garrett thought he heard a small sigh form somewhere behind him. He glanced around to find Catherine standing in the doorway to the terrace, her hand resting on her chest, and her eyes fixed on him. They stood for a moment transfixed.

Garrett was the first to break the spell. Turning fully to face her, he bowed low to Catherine. "Miss Elmsworth," he said in a low, steady voice. He didn't seem at all surprised to see her there.

"How good it is to see you. You look stunning this evening if I may be so bold in saying so." His lips formed a charming smile, bringing those delightful dimples into view.

"It is good to see you, too, Mr. Brennen," she replied. "It has been far too long since our encounter in the book shop. I hope you have been well."

"Very well, thank you. Lord and Lady Hawthorne have been kind enough to let me lodge with them while I am finishing my last term at Cambridge."

"Oh, I didn't know you were attending the university. I have friends who graduated from Cambridge last year. Perhaps you are acquainted with them. Lord Moreland? And his friends, Mr. James Worth and Mr. Arthur Fellows?"

"No, I do not believe I have had the pleasure of making their acquaintance," Garrett answered. "If they are academics, I am afraid our paths likely would not have crossed. Although I am studying the classics, as well as some mathematics, my primary area of interest is in music. I am studying under Professor William Bennett, the great pianist and composer.

"Of course," said Catherine. "You would not have been in the same circles as them."

"The same social circles, you mean?" asked Garrett a little harshly. "You think your friends are above me?"

"No," said Catherine. "I do not think that at all. If you knew me, Mr. Brennen, you would know that I do not put much stock into high society's standards and the separation of the classes. In fact, my very own parents defied the social edicts of their day by marrying in what was perceived by many as 'out of their class'."

Garrett took a few steps to bring him closer to her. "Interesting," he said, peering down at her with a glint in his eye and a sly smile. "And you, Miss Elmsworth, would you do the same?" He leaned in even closer. "Would you marry out of your class if it were true love?"

Catherine's gaze did not waver from his. She wanted to drown in those eyes. She wanted to throw herself into his arms and confess her love to him. She wanted to promise to love him and only him forever and ever, no matter what her Aunt Margaret, or Mary, or the *haut ton*, or anyone else had to say about it. She wanted to feel his luscious lips on hers.

"If I were to truly love someone," she said, her voice firm and full of passion, "Nothing nor no one could stop me from being with him." Her green eyes bore into his.

Garrett seemed as if he were about to say something. Tilting his head, a bit to one side, he then quickly stepped away from her and, laying his violin and bow on the stone bench, he retrieved his waistcoat. He had just put it on when Lady Hawthorne appeared next to Catherine.

"Catherine, dear, I do hope your dress was not ruined," she said. Then, noticing Garrett at the far end of the terrace, she first cast a curious glance at Catherine before turning her attention to Garrett. "There you are, Mr. Brennen," she said in a calm voice. "The guests have gathered in the music room if you are ready."

"Certainly, Lady Hawthorne, I will go there now." Bowing slightly toward them, he said, "Ladies, if you will excuse me."

"We will be right behind you, Mr. Brennen," said Lady Hawthorne. Taking Catherine's arm lightly, she added, "Shall we, Catherine?"

As they walked down the hall toward the music room, Catherine felt compelled to explain what she was doing on the terrace with Garrett, lest Lady Hawthorne get the wrong impression.

Casually she said, "I was hoping to get a bit a fresh air, when I came upon Mr. Brennen playing his violin on the terrace. I am afraid I got so caught up in the music, I quite forgot the impropriety of the situation, and since we are already acquainted, I saw no harm in saying hello when he had finished playing."

"Not to worry dear," Lady Hawthorne replied, squeezing Catherine's arm a wee bit tighter. "We are quite fond of Mr. Brennen, as we have had the opportunity to get to know him well in the last few months he has been staying with us. And I can truthfully attest to no wrongdoing going on as I came upon the two of you." She smiled reassuringly at Catherine. "If it troubles you, dear, no one ever need know about it."

"Oh no," Catherine assured her. "It does not trouble me at all. I was just a bit concerned about what others might think, especially Aunt Margaret. Unlike you, she is not very fond of Mr. Brennen."

"Perhaps that is just because she does not know him as my husband and I do," said Lady Hawthorne. "It may be that she will feel differently after tonight's performance." As they entered the music room, Lady Hawthorne led Catherine to two adjoining seats in the front row.

Taking her seat at the end of the row, Catherine watched Garrett as he prepared to play for the gathered guests. Lifting his violin gracefully to his shoulder, he gently stroked his bow over the strings. The music that poured forth was somber at first, then became filled with powerful emotions as he continued his earnest manipulation of his instrument. Closing his eyes, he seemed one with the instrument and the music emanating from it. He appeared lost in another world, one in which only he and the music existed.

Catherine felt lost, too, drawn in to the magic of the moment. She couldn't take her eyes from him. His beautiful hands caressing the instrument made her wish for those hands to be caressing her body in the same way, with such power and emotion, with such tenderness and obvious pleasure. Watching him play like that ignited something within her. Her body pulsed with sudden desire. Desire for him, desire to be touched and held and kissed by Garrett Brennen.

Garrett closed his eyes as he played. It helped him concentrate on the music. Tonight, though, his thoughts filled with Miss Elmsworth. When he had turned to see her standing in the doorway to the terrace, he had nearly dropped his violin. She was radiant in an emerald gown, with her lovely auburn locks, her fair skin, and her blazing green eyes. Eyes that pierced him to his soul and seemed to know him in a way he had never been known before. In a way he wished to be known by this woman.

It had taken him a moment to compose himself and step closer to her. As they spoke, he could think only of taking her in his arms. Her body seemed to call out to his in a way he had never experienced. It was all he could manage not to grab her and kiss her on the spot. He very nearly had, when he heard someone approaching from inside. He quickly stepped away from her and reached to retrieve his waistcoat, trying to calm the desire rushing through his body.

When Lady Hawthorne had appeared, he and Catherine stood at opposite ends of the terrace, and he was thankful nothing would seem amiss or be misinterpreted as indiscretion. It would have been quite the opposite, had he acted on his impulse to embrace Catherine. He must be careful when in her presence, so as not to act foolishly and bring dishonor or disgrace upon her. That was the last thing he wanted to do. He had to find a way to speak to her privately, though…to let her know who he really was…to tell her of his feelings for her.

Lost in her thoughts, Catherine hadn't realized the music had stopped until she heard the applause of the gathered guests. She glanced around the room, only to find Lord Harington staring at her. Scowling at him, Catherine turned her attention back to Garrett.

Bowing to his audience in gratitude of their applause, Garrett straightened and, smiling his beautiful, perfect dimpled smile, said, "I hope you will indulge me a little as I play an old tune that is a favorite of someone very special to me." As he placed the violin once more at his shoulder and leaned his cheek against the smooth wood, his eye met Catherine's for just a moment before he raised his bow and began playing 'Lady Greensleeves'.

It melted Catherine's heart to know that he remembered that tune as her favorite. And he had said it was a favorite of someone special to him. *Could he mean her? Was she special to him?* Catherine would give almost anything if she could just get up out of her seat right now and ask him. Of course, that would break every code of propriety there ever was, so she forced herself to remain seated. Still, the idea that Garrett might truly think of her as special touched her heart so that a warm flood of emotion spread through her entire body.

Garrett finished the tune with an ever so slight nod and the teensiest of smiles in her direction. Catherine's cheeks warmed slightly. Both of them hoped no one else in the room had noticed the brief exchange.

Garrett continued to entertain the guests for another half hour or so. They all seemed pleased with his performance, granting him a standing ovation at the end of it. It was true, he played very well. Though not yet a master, there was a certainty that he very well could be one day. His heart was certainly in it. If he could pursue a career in music, he could one day be the master, teaching other young men the skills of musicianship. If only he were at liberty to do so. Sadly, he was not. Other responsibilities awaited him back home, responsibilities he would one day be forced to give up his music in order to assume.

The guests began to disperse, some of them going forward to say a few words to Garrett before their departure. Catherine edged herself forward, aching to be near him for just a moment more. She was nearly there, when she felt a grab at her arm. She turned to find Aunt Margaret there, hand firmly clasped onto Catherine's arm.

"Come, Catherine," she said with firmness in her voice, "it is time for us to go."

"But, Aunt Margaret…" Catherine sputtered.

With a bit of force that was quite unlike her aunt, Catherine was pulled toward the door. With a backward glance, she caught Garrett watching the exchange, a frown on his face. With a final tug, her aunt whisked her away from him.

They quickly said their goodbyes to their hostess, Lady Hawthorne, and some of the other guests as they made their way to the door and their hasty departure. Once they were in the carriage and on their way home, Catherine addressed her aunt's odd behavior.

"Aunt Margaret, why were you in such a hurry to leave after the concert?" she prodded. "Surely, it was a bit rude to rush off like that, was it not?" Her aunt merely harrumphed in reply. Catherine pressed further. "I don't believe I have ever seen you behave is such a way, Aunt. There must have been a reason. Did something or someone offend you?"

Her features serious, Aunt Margaret peered at Catherine steadily. "The only offense, my dear, was that musician eyeing you the way he was."

"Whatever do you mean, Aunt? Gar-Mr. Brennen was doing no such thing," she replied adamantly. "Why, his eyes remained closed for most of the performance, so he couldn't possibly have been *eyeing* me as you say." *Surely, I would have noticed if he had been,* she mused to herself.

"I know what I saw, Catherine. From here on out, I want you to have absolutely no further contact with that young man," she said firmly.

Taken aback at her aunt's forcefulness, Catherine didn't know how to respond. After a moment, she said, "Surely, you are not suggesting, Aunt Margaret, that I lock myself in my room at home and never go to any of these social engagements you have be forcing me to attend." Her voice rose in indignation. "Shall I refuse all invitations from this day forward, supposing that there is a possibility Mr. Brennen could be at any one of them?"

Her aunt said stiffly, "I do not know what your fascination is with that young man, but I am certainly not going to encourage it." She leaned forward in her seat, ensuring Catherine was paying attention. "He is far beneath you, my dear, and pursuing any sort of intimacy, even if it is only an innocent friendship, is absolutely out of the question."

Catherine fought back tears at her aunt's horrid proclamation. The thought of never seeing Garrett again, or talking to him, was too much for her to bear.

Softening her voice a bit, Margaret continued. "Of course, I don't mean for you to be locked away in your room. You must attend these social events if you are to gain a husband." She peered out the window of the carriage and, speaking matter-of-factly, she added, "In fact, we are to attend a private dinner tomorrow night with the Lord and Lady Mosbey"

Catherine was suddenly alert. "A private dinner?" she asked. *Oh, dear,* she thought to herself. A private dinner with only Lord and

Lady Mosbey and their family, Aunt Margaret, and herself could only mean one thing. With his family's and Aunt Margaret's full support, Harry was going to declare his intentions.

"But, Aunt -," Catherine's protest was halted by Aunt Margaret's raised palm, and a brisk shake of her head.

"There will be no discussion on the matter, Catherine. You will attend the dinner and politely accept Harry's proposal."

Proposal! Oh no, it was even worse than she'd thought. Overcome with anxiety and torment, Catherine remained quiet the rest of the ride home. Thankfully, so did Aunt Margaret.

CHAPTER SEVEN

"For time will come with all its blights,
The ruined hope, the friend unkind,
And love, that leaves, wherever it lights,
A chilled or burning heart behind."
from *Whene'er I See Those Smiling Eyes*

The next evening, Lady Hathaway and Catherine arrived at the home of Lord and Lady Mosbey for dinner. Seated in the drawing room, Catherine tried to appear at ease as she conversed with Mary and Anna. Her pallor a bit ashen, and with the butterflies fluttering in her stomach making her feel a bit nauseous, she left it to the other girls to supply most of the conversation while she politely listened, occasionally nodding her head or smiling in agreement.

Once, she absentmindedly glanced up to find Harry staring at her. His eyes held adoration and tenderness. He smiled warmly at her. She could not bear it, nor return the smile, so she looked away abruptly. Her lips trembled, and she feared she might burst into tears, just as they were called in to dinner.

Of course, Harry rushed to her side, offering to escort her to the dining room. Catherine gamely placed her hand on his arm, but still refused to look at him as they made their way to table. She must gain control of herself and her emotions if she were to make it through this evening. As she seated herself, she took a deep breath, fortifying herself for what was to come.

She further fortified herself, and avoided much interaction with Harry, by busily occupying herself with the food that was placed in front of her. With gusto, she sampled everything before her, hoping to dissuade Harry's attempts at engaging her in conversation. She was uncomfortably stuffed by the time the dessert was served.

As the women disbursed back to the drawing room, Harry followed his father to the library. A short time later, they both appeared at the drawing room door. Looking a bit sheepish, Harry stepped forward toward Catherine. With a hopeful look on his face, he asked, "Catherine, might I have a word with you... in private."

Her eyes racing blindly around the room, they fixated on Aunt Margaret, who gave a little nod.

Catherine rose from her seat without a word and proceeded to follow Harry out of the room and down the hall to the library. Seating herself in one of the comfortable, oversized chairs, Catherine glanced around the room. *Why the library?* she found herself thinking. *Must we have this dreadful conversation in the library of all rooms?* She fervently hoped it would not ruin libraries for her in the future.

Sitting in silence, she waited as Harry seated himself in the chair next to hers. She still refused to look at him. Her hands shook, and she clasped them firmly in her lap. She sat there, a frozen lump, her eyes fastened on them, willing Harry not to say the words she was sure were soon to come.

"Catherine." He spoke her name softly. Catherine still did not move or look at him. Harry reached out and, gently prying one of her hands free, clasped it in his. "Catherine", he repeated, this time with more urgency in his voice.

Catherine forced herself to raise her head. She saw the earnestness in Harry's eyes. He smiled at her reassuringly. Then with a slight chuckle, he said, "You don't have to look so fearful, Catherine, I'm not going to hurt you."

Smiling awkwardly, Catherine tried to calm her nerves. The butterflies were wreaking havoc in her gut. She began to fear she might cast up her accounts all over Harry's boots. That would make this whole ordeal so much more horrible. She absolutely must gain control of herself if she were to get through this. She looked at Harry. Smiling weakly, she waited for him to speak again.

"Catherine," he once more attempted. "You and I have been acquainted for some time now, and I believe we have become good friends." He paused, allowing her time to respond. When she offered no response, Harry continued. "In the time we have spent together, it has been my fervent hope that our friendship might grow into something more."

Growing a bit frustrated at the lack of response or acknowledgement from Catherine, Harry proceeded. "You must know I have feelings for you, Catherine, which are completely unfriend like." With his free hand Harry lightly touched Catherine's chin, drawing her eyes up to meet his.

"I wish to marry you," he said.

At Catherine's refusal to engage in this conversation, Harry dropped his hand and released his hold on hers. Sighing heavily, he turned away slightly.

Catherine felt a sudden compassion for him. He was a good man, Harry was, and a good friend, but she could not bring herself to agree to become his wife. She just could not. She did not love him, at least not in the way a woman should love a husband. Besides, how could she even consider marrying another when her heart lay elsewhere? She could not do that to Harry, nor to any man she did not love. And she loved only one man. She loved Garrett. Of that she had never been more sure.

She felt some guilt over what she knew she must say to Harry. He deserved an answer though it would not be the answer he sought. Leaning toward him, Catherine gently placed her hand on his arm.

"Harry," she began hesitantly. "You are a wonderful and charming man, and you have been a dear friend."

Harry bowed his head, anticipating her rejection. Taking his hand in hers and willing him to look at her, Catherine continued.

"I am truly sorry, Harry, but I feel it would not be kind or just of me to accept your proposal of marriage when I do not share the same feelings as you."

Harry turned away from her, and Catherine was sure she saw him blinking back tears.

"Do forgive me, Harry," she said softly. "I would hate for this to bring ruin to our friendship, as I do value it so greatly."

Gaining his composure, Harry rose from his chair. Drawing himself up to his full height, his back straight, he faced Catherine. With a great sigh, he said, "I know you only have eyes for one man, Catherine, but surely you must know that you can never have him." He turned to leave, then hesitating, he turned back to her. "You would do yourself well to set your sights elsewhere," he said before exiting the room.

After the disastrous proposal dinner, Catherine found those whom she had once called friends now seemed to be taking great care to avoid her. Harry's reluctance to be around her she could understand, but Mary had become her close friend, as close as Catherine would let her be anyway. There were things Catherine had not confided to Mary or anyone else. Like the way she felt about Garrett Brennen, for one. No one could know that. If her aunt knew, there was no telling what she would do, probably send Catherine off to live with nuns, or some other such extreme measure.

And the *ton?* Lord, if they were to find out, she would be cast out from them post haste. She wouldn't mind that so much, come to think of it. Catherine did not wish to be like them. She was thankful she had had the upbringing her aunt had provided for her and all she had learned about being a lady. However, she did not like to exclude someone from her friendship merely because she'd had the good fortune to have been brought up thusly.

It burdened her heart that some people, people who worked as servants, and people who labored for the benefit of others, were treated so brutishly by high society members. Her aunt wasn't like that, at least for the most part. She had always treated her staff with kindness and generosity, like they were real people, human beings just like the rest of us.

When it came down to it though, the reality was Aunt Margaret did fancy herself better than them. She fell right in with the *beau monde* in excluding all those beneath her, even handsome, young, and very talented musicians. Catherine, herself would not be a part of it, even if it meant her own exclusion from high society. She would follow her heart and love whomever she was meant to love. If only she could find a way to do so without bringing shame and dishonor upon her aunt.

"Catherine!" her aunt shouted shrilly. Catherine ran down the stairs to find Aunt Margaret standing in the foyer, with a piece of paper in her hand.

"What is it Aunt Margaret?" asked Catherine with some urgency as she rushed to her aunt's side. "Has something happened?"

Waving the paper frantically in front of her, Aunt Margaret turned to her, her face alight with exertion. "*Something* is about to happen, my dear," she exclaimed. "Lord Harington is having a ball! *And* it is to be a masquerade ball!" Her eyes dance merrily, as if this were the most wonderful news she had ever received.

Catherine refrained from rolling her eyes. "Auntie, you frightened me with alarm," she said in a serious tone. "I thought something terrible had happened. And you're telling me you are this frantic about a ball?" Sighing heavily, she turned to retrace her steps back up to her room.

Following closely behind her, Margaret continued to wave the invitation. "Not just *any* ball, Catherine, a masked ball. And at Lord Harington's mansion," she added wistfully. Why, this is *the* invitation of the season." Stopping at the foot of the stairs, Margaret frowned at her niece dejectedly. "I should think

111

you would be pleased at such an invitation. Everyone who is anyone will be there," she said.

"Precisely why I am not overly excited at the prospect of attending, Auntie," Catherine replied sourly, turning to continue up the stairs.

"You have been taught, Catherine, and would do well to put into practice, the manners befitting your station. You will learn, young lady, that there is much to be gained by ingratiating oneself into society," she said to Catherine's retreating back. "Even if it is not one's greatest desire to do so," she added with emphasis.

The masked ball was just one week away. Catherine had chosen a deep magenta gown for the occasion. Her aunt had purchased wigs and masks for them. The wigs were both white, with the hair piled high and many adornments attached. Catherine's mask was the same deep shade as her dress, with gold trim. There were black feathers attached at the sides. Though hers was only a half-mask, when Catherine tried it on, she found she enjoyed the anonymity the mask afforded. It felt a bit sensual and clandestine. She enjoyed the feeling. Despite her initial misgivings, she found herself looking forward to the ball with anticipation.

Catherine sat in the library, trying to lose herself in a good book. Instead, she daydreamed. She thought about Garrett Brennen. It had been weeks since she'd seen him last. She wondered if he would be at the masquerade ball. Catherine was certain Lord Harington would have an orchestra playing rather than just a few musicians. Surely, Garrett would be among those hired to play for the evening.

Catherine hoped with all her heart he would be there. She wanted so desperately to speak with him. She was ready to tell him how she felt about him, high society be damned. She didn't care what anyone else thought, she loved him, and she wanted him to know it. In her heart, she was certain he felt the same for her. She let herself be carried away with thoughts of being held in Garrett's arms, thoughts of his warm, passionate lips on hers. To her way of thinking, there could be nothing finer than to love and be loved by Garrett Brennen.

CHAPTER EIGHT

"Oh! yes, so well, so tenderly
Thou art loved, adored by me,
Fame, fortune, wealth, and liberty,
Were worthless without thee."
from *Oh! Yes, So Well*

The night of the masquerade ball, Abby helped Catherine into her lovely magenta gown. Carefully pinning up her auburn locks, Abby gingerly set the wig atop Catherine's head. It felt a bit heavy, and Catherine hoped it wouldn't cause her neck to ache as the evening progressed. She was a bit worried about her ability to dance with it on as well. She hoped she could manage it without too much difficulty. Picking up her mask, Catherine went to join her aunt, and they were soon on their way.

Alighting from the carriage once they had arrived, Catherine marveled at Lord Harington's mansion. It was certainly immense, that was true. Catherine wondered what, or who, occupied all those rooms. Whatever did one need such huge living quarters for? Especially when the one was a bachelor?

Putting on her mask, Catherine followed Aunt Margaret into the spacious foyer. As the ladies entered the ballroom, Catherine's heart danced in anticipation. She was positive she would be seeing Garrett tonight, and she couldn't wait. She hurriedly scanned the huge room. There it was, the small enclosure at one end that would contain the night's musicians. When she saw that all the seats were filled and no Garrett, her heart sank. The other young violinist, the one she'd seen at the Marquess and Marchioness Hawthorne's ball, was there, but another young man was seated next to him, a man who was not Garrett.

Seeing Lord Harington approaching them, Catherine tried to hide her disappointment. She was thankful she wore a mask, hoping that no one would be able to see the hurt she bore. She had been so sure this would be the night she and Garrett confessed their love for one another.

"Lady Hathaway," said Lord Harington, recognizing her aunt right away since she had forgotten to put on her mask. Eyeing Catherine, he teased, "and who might this lovely lady be?"

"Lord Harington," Catherine said, nodding in acknowledgement. "Thank you so much for inviting us."

"We have been looking forward to this evening with much anticipation, Lord Harington," said Margaret. "Catherine has been quite beside herself, so much has she been looking forward to it."

Catherine looked at her aunt incredulously. *What? I was no such thing,* thought Catherine. *What is she up to now?*

Brooks stared at Catherine, a strange, somewhat surprised, yet questioning, look on his face. "I hope it meets all your expectations, Miss Elmsworth," he said.

"I hope so as well, my lord." Catherine replied.

"Oh, there are Lord and Lady Hawthorne!" Aunt Margaret exclaimed. "Do excuse me Lord Harington while I say how do you do to them." Giving Catherine a pointed look, off she went to greet her friends.

After a brief moment in which neither spoke, Lord Harington asked, "Miss Elmsworth, may I have the honor of the first dance of the evening?"

"Of course, my lord," Catherine answered. At that moment, the first dance was announced. Placing her hand upon the earl's outstretched arm, Catherine allowed him to lead her onto the dance floor. His gaze remained upon her as they danced, so much so, that Catherine began to grow a bit nervous under the intensity of it.

"May I say, Miss Elmsworth," Brooks said as the dance brought them close in proximity to one another, "that you look quite lovely this evening." Smiling down at her, he added, "The parts of you I can see, at least. I can only imagine the beauty hidden behind the mask," he whispered as they drew near to one another.

Catherine was aghast. How dare he speak to her in such a manner, making such an intimate reference to her person.

"I have offended you," he said. "Please forgive me. It was not my intent."

"Perhaps, my lord, it would be best if we continue the remainder of the dance in silence."

"As you wish, Miss Elmsworth."

No other words were spoken between them until the dance ended. Catherine curtseyed. "Thank you, Lord Harington," she said.

"Miss Elmsworth," he replied with a slight nod. "It was my great pleasure."

Another man in a mask approached as Lord Harington took his leave.

"My lady," said the newcomer. "Might I have the honor of the next dance?"

Catherine looked at him, incredulous. "My lord, surely you know how unseemly it would be for a young lady to be caught dancing with a man she has not yet been properly introduced to."

"But we have been introduced, Catherine," he replied, lifting his hand to raise his mask. "It is I, James Worth."

"James!" Catherine said excitedly. "You have returned!"

"Yes, I have been back for a week's time." The music began again. Gesturing toward the other couples occupying the dance floor, James asked, "Shall we?"

As they danced, they were able to carry on somewhat of a conversation.

"I have been to see Harry," James said tentatively.

"And how did you find him?" asked Catherine.

"In honesty, I found him a bit broken-hearted," James answered, "but recovering well I believe."

Catherine gave no reply.

"You needn't trouble yourself over it, my lady," James encouraged. "Harry is a good man, and he will one day find himself a good woman to love. Someone who can love him in return."

"I do hope you are right, James," Catherine quietly replied. "I do wish only the best for him. As you say, he is a good man."

The dance ended, and they stood together, talking. "And what of Anna?" Catherine asked. "Were you able to see her as well, when you visited Harry?"

James' eyebrows rose just above his mask, in a look of surprise. "Anna?" was all he said.

Smiling, Catherine replied, "Surely, James, you must know she is quite infatuated with you."

When James stood frozen and unresponsive, Catherine's brow furrowed, and her mouth turned down in a frown. "I thought there was a mutual attraction, James. Please forgive me if I am wrong in my assumption."

After a slight pause, James said, "No...no, you are not wrong, Catherine. It's just that I was not aware anyone knew, that is all. Did Anna tell you, or do others know as well?"

"I observed some silent communication between the two of you during the dinner at the home of Lord and Lady Mosbey. When I spoke to Anna later that evening, she told me. It appears she has been quite taken with you for some time." Concerned that her young friend, or as it appeared now, *ex*-friend, was imagining James' return of her affection, Catherine pursued the matter. "James," she said in a serious tone, "You do care about her, do you not?"

James smiled. "Yes, Miss Elmsworth, I am afraid I am quite smitten with the young lady." Relaxing his stance a little, he said, "You know, while I was visiting my family, all I kept hearing from all of them was 'When will you find a wife, James?', 'What are you waiting for, James?' etcetera, etcetera. I could not say to them, 'I am waiting patiently for the love of my life to turn sixteen, so I may finally be able to court her.'" Sheepishly, he added, "Rest assured, Catherine, I intend to be most honorable in every respect. It is just that it is hard on a man to have to wait to be with his true love."

Catherine grew thoughtful. "Yes, I suppose it is," she said, "Just as it is hard on a woman to have to wait to be with hers."

Looking wistfully off into the distance, Catherine was not even aware of the curious look James cast her way. "Please excuse me, James," she said flatly as she walked away.

Catherine needed to be alone. She had lost her heart to a mysterious young musician, and now she wondered if she would ever see him again. She had so hoped he would be here tonight, and her hopes had been dashed to the ground. She felt as if she would burst into tears at any moment. She needed to find a private place where she could be alone with her aching heart. As she was making her way to the door, she felt a hand grab her arm.

"Miss Elmsworth?" the gentleman said, his hand still grasping her arm.

"Please excuse me," she said, pulling her arm free. She turned to go.

"Catherine…wait."

Hearing the slight lilt when he said her name, she turned back to face him. He, too, wore a white wig, but his was a full face mask, so she could see nothing of his features. *Could it be?* Her eyes met his, and then she knew. There was no other man of her acquaintance with eyes like those…amber orbs that sparked when he looked at her. Bringing her hand to her mouth, she whispered in disbelief, "Garrett?"

The gentleman bowed slightly in acknowledgement. "Catherine," he answered, his voice deep and resonant. "Please, don't go…stay…dance with me." He held out his hand to her.

Slipping her hand into his, Catherine felt the warmth flow through her entire body. When they reached the dance floor, the waltz was just beginning. As they danced, their eyes remained fixed on each other. The other couples, the crowd, the music, all seemed to disappear. It was just the two of them, dancing together.

"Are you surprised to see me, lass?" he asked with a twinkle in his eye.

"I confess, it was my hope that I would see you here tonight," she said with a timid smile. "When I did not find you in the orchestra, that hope faded. How did you manage to get in here, Mr. Brennen? This is a private ball, and," she hesitated to say it, but continued, "I am quite certain you were not invited."

"You are quite correct, my lady. To my great misfortune, Lord Harington did indeed show some neglect in sending me an invitation." His eyes danced merrily with mirth. "However," he continued, "when the ball is a masquerade ball, it increases the chances of one being able to slip in undetected."

A laugh escaped Catherine's lips. "You sneaked in?" she asked. "You took a great risk in doing so. Garrett, what if you were to be found out?" she asked nervously. "I do not believe Lord Harington is a man who would treat such a thing lightly," she said. "Why ever would you take such a risk?"

"Why, to see you, of course," said Garrett in all seriousness. "And to dance with you, my sweet, dear Catherine," he whispered, as his lips brushed against her ear, sending a vein of fire through her body. "How else would I ever have been able to do so? Your aunt has forbidden me to see you."

The words he spoke filled Catherine with such happiness, she couldn't keep the smile from her face as they danced. Each time they touched, however briefly, she felt as if her entire body was alight and alive. All too soon, though, the music ended. Catherine longed to continue dancing with him, to spend more time just being in his presence, but she knew that to do so would draw undesired attention to them both.

Catherine looked up to see Lord Harington watching them, a frown upon his face, as he spoke to a man standing near him. When the man turned to look their way, Catherine knew they were discussing the man she danced with, probably trying to deduce who he was.

"I think you'd better make yourself scarce, Mr. Brennen," she whispered quietly. "It seems we have drawn the attention of our host."

Without turning to look in Lord Harington's direction, Garrett briefly clasped Catherine's gloved hand and bowed slightly to her, whispering, "Meet me on the terrace." He smiled up at her, then stood back up to take his leave. Before he turned from her, he said, "I'll wait for you." He quickly disappeared in the crowd.

A moment later, Lord Harington was at her side. "Who was that man you were dancing with, Catherine?" She heard the disapproval in his voice.

"Why, I couldn't say, my lord," Catherine answered, turning to face him. "I did not recognize him with the mask on. Do you not know him, Lord Harington?"

Rubbing his chin, he pondered a moment before answering. "He did seem a bit familiar, but I can't recall inviting anyone who is not well known to me."

"I'm afraid I cannot be of much help to you, my lord, as most of the people here are not yet well known to me." Turning away slightly to hide her smile, she added, "He was rather charming a fellow, though."

"It seems we are destined to keep meeting on terraces, Mr. Brennen."

"It seems, my lady, that meeting on terraces is the only way that affords us any privacy."

"And pray tell, Mr. Brennen, what might we have need of privacy for?" Catherine teased.

Taking two long, quick strides, Garrett closed the distance between them, removing his mask as he did so. His penetrating gaze made Catherine's knees go weak, and her heartbeat quicken. Her eyes didn't leave his. What she saw there, in those heated amber irises, reflected what she herself was feeling at that moment…desire.

A tiny gasp escaped Catherine's throat when Garrett reached for her and, pulled her to him. Lifting her mask, his eyes moved over her features, leaving a warm trail as they did. She watched as they left her eyes and flowed over her cheeks, down to her chin, resting finally on her lips. She wanted more than just his gaze touching her lips. *Please, oh please, kiss me!* Her thoughts begged.

Before she knew what was happening, his mouth was on hers, and oh, it was heaven! The touch of his lips against hers, somehow urgent and gentle at the same time; the taste of him; the strength of his arms around her all worked together till Catherine felt as if she would melt into a puddle right there at Garrett's feet.

A low, deep moan, coming from the back of his throat, assured Catherine that Garrett was enjoying the kiss as much as she. Seconds later, though, he stopped kissing her and pulled abruptly away from her, leaving Catherine feeling cold and empty where she had just felt full and warm.

"I am so sorry, Catherine, please forgive me," said Garrett, refusing to meet her eyes. He paced a few steps away from her, then turned and paced back. He looked at her, his eyes dark and serious. "I should not have done that," he said. "I had no right to do that!" he spoke roughly in anger, more to himself than to her.

Catherine reached out and tentatively put her hand on his shoulder. "Garrett," she said softly as if trying to calm a beast. "You did nothing wrong. I wanted that kiss." *My body was begging for it,* she added in her own thoughts. "I have wanted it since I first met you in the Meriwether's foyer." She added with a shy smile. "In fact, had you not kissed me at that exact moment, I am quite certain I would have embarrassed myself immensely by grabbing you in an embrace and kissing you," she said, trying to lighten the sudden dark mood.

She peered up at him, forcing him to look at her. "Garrett, there is something I must tell you."

She had something she must tell him? thought Garrett. He had things he needed to say to her as well. Now was the time for him to make his confession. Catherine had given him the perfect opening to tell her the truth about who he was.

Pulling her body up against his, Catherine leaned in and, looking longingly into his eyes, she whispered, "I love you, Garrett."

Garrett pushed Catherine away from him none too gently. "No!...No, don't say that Catherine."

His eyes filled with such sadness, Catherine feared he might actually shed tears.

"You can't mean it," he said, shaking his head back and forth. "You don't even know me, Catherine." He turned away from her and moved over to the terrace wall, where he stood with his back to her, looking out into the night.

"I know my heart, Garrett Brennen," Catherine said fiercely. "And my heart knows you. *I know you*...well enough to know that I never wish to be parted from you."

"Catherine, please stop!" he said forcefully, turning back to face her. "You have no idea what you are saying, or who you are saying it to. I am not who you think I am," he finished in a quieter tone.

Suddenly, there were voices drawing near. Catherine turned in the direction of the sounds, but all she saw was darkness. When she turned back, Garrett was gone. Catherine moved to the edge of the terrace and peered out into the darkness. She saw and heard nothing. She wanted to call out into the darkness but was afraid it would draw unwanted attention.

Catherine stood for a moment puzzling over what Garrett had said. *What could he mean, he is not who I think he is? And how could it make any difference anyway? My heart is already his no matter who he might be.*

Looking around the terrace once more but finding no trace of Garrett, Catherine slowly made her way back inside. Just inside the door, she encountered Lord Harington.

"Are you unwell, Catherine?" he asked, grasping her elbow lightly to steady her. "You look a bit faint. Do you need to sit down?" he asked, his voice laced with concern.

"Yes, thank you, my lord. I think maybe I do need to sit for just a bit."

Seeing her to a nearby chair, and ensuring she was safely seated and not about to topple over, Brooks said, "Let me fetch you something to drink. I will return momentarily." He departed toward the refreshment table.

Catherine glanced around the room, only half seeing the crowd before her. The ladies in their brightly colored gowns and masks appeared to Catherine like a rainbow entwining itself throughout the room. The gentlemen, most of them dressed in darker colors and more sedate masks, were like dark clouds floating through the rainbow. The whole scene appeared somewhat ethereal to Catherine. She began to fear she really would faint. Then Lord Harington was back at her side, offering her a glass of cool lemonade.

Taking the glass from him, careful not to spill anything on her gown, Catherine took a long drink. With a sigh, she sat back in her chair as the room began to come into focus once again.

"Thank you, Brooks," she said, forgetting for a moment where they were and whom they were amongst. Catherine looked up at him. The creases of concern across his forehead had softened a bit, but he still seemed reluctant to leave her side. "I am fine, now, my lord, you need not hover as if I am some invalid," she said lightly.

When Brooks showed no intention of leaving her side, Catherine persisted. "Please, Lord Harington, surely you have need to attend to your other guests. I can assure you, I am truly fine, and I do sincerely thank you for your concern, and for the drink." She raised her glass to him, smiling, and took another sip.

"Very well, Miss Elmsworth, I will take my leave. Before I do, though, may I fetch your aunt for you?"

"No, no, there is no need for that, my lord. You would only alarm her." With a small smirk, she added, "Besides, you have done quite enough 'fetching' for me tonight. You are the host after all, you should not be the one 'fetching' anything."

Catherine could swear she saw the side of his mouth raise in a constrained smile. "As you wish, Catherine," he said with a bow, before going off to join a group of men who had gathered some distance from her.

After resting a few more minutes, Catherine got up from her seat and began to walk around the ballroom. She peered between the small groups congregating on the outskirts of the dance floor. She watched the couples dancing, her eyes searching. She knew what, or *whom* she was searching for, but he was nowhere to be found. It seemed as if he had disappeared just as quickly as he had appeared.

As Catherine stood off to the side of the room, deep in her own thoughts, she tried to sort out her feelings regarding the happenings of this evening. She had started the evening high in anticipation of seeing Garrett, but when it appeared he wasn't going to show, disappointment had overwhelmed her. There was the great surprise when she found them dancing together, and then…there was the kiss on the terrace, which brought a whole new set of emotions Catherine had never experienced before.

She would never have dreamed that one kiss could hold so much passion and longing smoldering within it. Or that Garrett's body pressing into hers could create such a flow of heat through her entire body. Or that the heat could be removed just as quickly. He'd acted so harshly, pushing her away, and refusing her confession of her love for him.

Whatever could that be about? she pondered. She had been certain Garrett felt the same way for her as she felt for him. As she stood there, trying to make some sense of it, a man approached her. He wore a half mask much like Catherine's, though with much less adornment than her own. Catherine could not make out who he was.

"Might I have the pleasure of this dance, Miss Elmsworth? It is Miss Elmsworth, isn't it?" he inquired, his lips twitching in mirth, as he teased.

The voice was vaguely familiar. Still not sure who he was, Catherine replied, "If I am to agree to a dance with you, sir, I must first know who it is I shall be agreeing to dance with."

"My lady, surely you have not completely forgotten all of your former friends so quickly after breaking the heart of one of them."

Harry? No, not Harry, for she would surely know him. Who then? Suddenly, it came to her.

"Ah, Mr. Fellows," she said triumphantly. "How good of you and Mr. Worth to continue your acquaintance with me when Harry and his sisters refuse to," said Catherine as she accepted his outstretched arm, and they joined the other dancers already in their places.

With a broad smile, Arthur said, "My dear Miss Elmsworth, I would never let my friends, or anyone else, dictate with whom I should be acquainted, and most definitely not when the person in question is a beautiful young lady."

"Your attempt at flattery will attain little success with me, I am afraid, Mr. Fellows, for I am not easily swayed by such flowery words. However, I must say that I do agree with you in regard to letting the opinions or rationale of others dictate who one might choose to be acquainted with. I, myself, feel very strongly in favor of making one's own choices in the matter of acquaintances and friendships."

"You sound as if you have had similar experience in the matter," said Arthur.

"I have," said Catherine. "Only recently, my aunt has forbidden me to become acquainted with someone." Realizing what she had just confided in Arthur Fellows of all people, Catherine tried to cover her slip by redirecting the conversation.

"Mr. Fellows," she began tentatively, "how is it that you have not found a wife yet?" Catherine knew the best way to distract Arthur was to get him talking about his favorite subject – himself.

"There are just so many beautiful and charming women here in London, Miss Elmsworth, that I find it quite impossible to choose just one," he answered, smiling broadly. "And there is the sad fact I have been told that your heart has already been engaged elsewhere," he added, offering her his most charming smile.

"Where did you hear such a thing, Mr. Fellows?" she exclaimed. "I have made no such claim."

"But it is true, is it not?" he persisted. "I have it on good authority."

"By whose authority?" she asked, indignant. When Arthur refused to answer, she supposed that it must have been Harry who had told him. Calmly, she replied, "I can assure you that whatever you may have heard should not be taken too seriously, especially when it appears the information you received may have come from someone whose own attentions may have been recently rejected."

With a smirk, Arthur answered, "No need to get upset, my lady. Forget I mentioned it." With the dance just ending, Arthur continued, "Let's call a truce, Catherine. I should like it if we could end the dance, and the evening, on good terms."

"As long as you promise not to repeat what I have told you is not true, then I will agree to a truce and we may part as friends."

"Done," said Arthur, extending his hand. Catherine allowed him to clasp hers, which he bowed low over. "You have my word, my lady."

"Then I bid you goodnight, Mr. Fellows."

Goodnight to you, Miss Elmsworth."

"Well, Catherine, it is nice to see that you have remained friends with Mr. Fellows despite the breech of friendship with Harry and his sisters," Aunt Margaret observed as she came to stand beside Catherine.

"Yes, I was pleasantly surprised to find that both Mr. Worth and Mr. Fellows seem unaffected by the indelicate business with Harry. I was approached by each of them for a dance, and they were both very friendly and kind."

"I am glad to hear it," Margaret replied. "One cannot afford to alienate what few single men there are in London this season. Not if one hopes to be able to find a suitable husband among them."

Catherine opened her mouth to protest, but her aunt waved for her to follow, saying, "Come along, Catherine. This old woman has reached her limit and wishes to retire. Let us find our host and thank him for a lovely evening before we take our leave."

The Earl's Masquerade

CHAPTER NINE

"It came o'er her sleep,
like a voice of those days,
When love, only love,
was the light of her ways;
And, soft as in moments of bliss long ago,
It whispered her name from the garden below."
from *The Voice; from (Legendary Ballads)*

Days and weeks passed after the night of the ball with no sign of Garrett. Catherine grew sullen. She moped around the house, occasionally strolling in the garden, and was generally surly to nearly everyone she encountered.

The few parties Aunt Margaret had insisted she attend had done nothing to lighten Catherine's mood. She was cordial, but only just enough so that people would not question her moodiness. She refrained from most conversation, only nodding here and there, adding an 'mm-hmm' or some other mummer of agreement.

Her heart just wasn't in it. Her heart was somewhere else...with Garrett, wherever he was. Catherine had not seen nor heard any word of him or his whereabouts since the night of the masquerade when he had vanished without a word.

After weeks of silence, Mary came to call. Catherine was surprised and happy to see her friend. After a few awkward moments of initial unease, they both relaxed and fell into the comfortable companionship they had once shared. Mary informed Catherine that Harry had apparently transferred his affections elsewhere, and since he bore no grudge against Catherine, Mary saw no reason why she should either. They were once again spending much of their time in the company of one another.

Aunt Margaret had invited some of her lady friends to tea one afternoon. Catherine was pleased to see that among them was Lady Hawthorne. Perhaps, during the course of their conversation, she might divulge some information regarding her house guest, Mr. Brennen. Catherine was desperate for some word of him. She listened attentively as the ladies talked, hoping to hear some mention of him. She waited in vain, however.

The tea time passed quickly, and the ladies were soon gathering their cloaks and shawls preparing to take their leave. Catherine could not let Lady Hawthorne leave without at least an attempt to gain some information from her, no matter how small it might be. As Aunt Margaret accompanied the other guests to the door, Catherine delayed Lady Hawthorne. Though it might be considered very improper behavior on her part, Catherine had to make the inquiry.

"Lady Hawthorne," she began, hesitantly. "How is your house guest, Mr. Brennen, getting along? I have not noticed him performing at any of the parties of late. I hope all is well."

"I am afraid Mr. Brennen is no longer our guest," Lady Hawthorne replied. "He was called away back to Ireland some weeks ago. A family matter, I believe." Turning to take her leave, she added, "He was such a charming young man. I admit I was sorry to see him go."

Without thinking, Catherine blurted, "Do you think he will be back?"

Lady Hawthorne stopped and gave Catherine a puzzled look at her outburst of impropriety. "Why, I wouldn't know, my dear," she said, primly. "I didn't think it proper to make such an inquiry upon his timely departure. If I were to wager a guess in the matter, I would say that we will probably not have the good fortune of his company again. At least, not any time in the near future," she said. "Good day, Catherine."

"Good day, Lady Hawthorne," Catherine returned. "It was a pleasure to see you."

Dismayed and heartbroken at the news of Garrett's departure, Catherine grew even more sullen and withdrawn. Both Mary and Aunt Margaret worked at persuading her to go out on occasion, but she did so with great reluctance. It was at one such event, a large garden party, that she was approached by Lord Harington.

"Miss Elmsworth," he said as he approached. "It is a pleasure to see you as always. It has been quite some time since our last meeting. It was at the masquerade if I remember correctly."

"Yes, my lord, you are correct." Catherine forced a smile. Though she was somewhat pleased to see him again, she struggled to find even a small amount of joy in anything these days.

Sensing her unease with the large crowd, Lord Harington asked, "I wonder, my lady, would you like to join me for a walk...a stroll in the garden perhaps?"

"Yes," Catherine nearly sighed with relief. "That would be lovely, thank you." She felt a rush of gratitude as he led her away from the group. Though they remained within sight of the others, they walked some distance away where it was quieter and much more peaceful.

After a few minutes, Brooks broke the silence. "I have heard from your aunt that you have not been feeling well of late. I hope that has changed and you are feeling better now."

"My aunt may be overstating it a bit," replied Catherine with a small smile. "I have been a bit melancholy is all. It is not my natural state to engage in so much social activity, and I am afraid all of the parties and social events I have been urged to attend have worn me down a bit."

"I apologize if my asking to walk with you and engaging you in conversation contributes in any way to your discomfort," Brooks urgently responded.

"There is no need for apology, my lord. I much prefer being in the company and conversation with one person, rather than in a group of people." Turning toward him and raising her head to look up at him, Catherine offered him a smile, and this time it was a genuine one.

"In fact," she admitted, "I believe I should thank you for drawing me away from that crowd." Glancing around her, she breathed deep, taking in the flowery scents. "I do love walking in the garden," she confessed. "It and reading are two of my greatest pleasures," she continued, "and when done together, they bring me great joy."

"I also enjoy reading as a pastime," Brooks remarked. "I don't believe we have ever discussed the topic of books before, Miss Elmsworth. What is it you like best to read?" he asked.

Catherine thought for a moment how to answer. Would he find her foolish if she admitted she had a fondness for novels? Most men thought them a very low form of writing as well as reading. Catherine decided she wished to be honest in her dealings with Brooks. He seemed to command that of her.

"While I admit I do enjoy a good novel or biography, my reading preference is poetry," Catherine offered, half-expecting him to dismiss both as useless drivel.

"Ah, poetry, the language of love," mused Brooks. "Is there a particular poet whose work you enjoy?" he asked with sincerity.

Catherine was a bit taken aback by his seeming interest. Surely, he was just trying to be accommodating to the conversation and had no real interest in what poet she favored.

"At the moment, I am quite fond of Thomas Moore's work," replied Catherine. "Do you know of him?" she asked.

"The Irish poet?" Brooks responded. "Yes, I am familiar with his work."

"I particularly enjoy his love poems," Catherine elaborated. "They are so full of passion and endearment, one cannot possibly read them and doubt the existence of true love."

"Do you doubt the existence of love, Catherine?" Brooks asked softly.

Catherine felt her blasted cheeks coloring at the direction their conversation was suddenly taking. Unable to respond immediately, she took a deep breath, composing herself.

"Not at all, my lord," she answered. "I firmly believe in the existence of love."

"And what of true love, then, my lady?" he probed. "Do you believe there is but one true love for each person?"

Catherine's thoughts turned to Garrett and she grew quiet. "I confess, my lord, that I am not sure what I believe regarding one true love."

"You have never experienced it then," he asked. "True love, I mean."

How is it possible I am having this conversation with Lord Harington of all people? Catherine asked herself. What was it about this man that compelled her to honesty and transparency in all things?

"I..," Catherine hesitated. "I did, yes," she said softly. "At least I thought it was true love at the time." Shaking her head slightly, she added, "Now, I am not so sure it was."

They came upon a stone bench along the walkway. Gesturing for her to sit, Brooks sat next to her. He grew serious and quiet. "What changed your thinking?" he asked.

Catherine had never spoken to anyone about her feelings for Garrett and the ache she still carried in her heart for him. Yet, Lord Harington seemed so sincere in his probing for answers, in his desire to know her, that she felt herself opening up to him, letting him in to the deepest parts of herself, parts she had never shared with anyone…parts she had wanted so desperately to share with Garrett.

"It is hard to say," answered Catherine. "The relationship was cut short before it ever had a chance to begin, really." She paused, deep in her own thoughts. "There were circumstances that arose which could not be avoided, nor changed."

"That is unfortunate," Brooks sympathized. He placed his hand gently...tentatively...briefly over hers. "I am sorry that such suffering was brought upon you, Catherine." Removing his hand, he said, "Were there anything I could do to change it, be assured that I would do so without a moment's hesitation."

Touched by his impassioned declaration and the sincerity with which he spoke it, Catherine looked up at him and smiled. "I appreciate your kind thoughtfulness, Lord Harington, but sadly, I am afraid there is nothing that can be done. It is over and finished," she spoke the words with finality, perhaps hoping to convince herself they were true. Turning to face him, she inquired, "And what of you, my lord, have you ever experienced true love?"

"I have not," he replied, "though I have great hope that it will happen one day." Gazing down at her, he added, "perhaps for both of us."

After a few more quiet moments, Brooks arose from the bench, reaching out to assist Catherine.

"Shall we make our way back, my lady, before our separation from the group becomes suspicious? I would not want to illicit any improper imaginings in the minds of the other guests," he said with a slight grin.

"Of course, my lord," Catherine agreed, taking his hand and standing. "We most certainly would not want to start the rumors flying about now would we?"

They walked down the path back toward the group in silence. As they neared the end of the path, Brooks spoke.

"Catherine, I have quite enjoyed our walk, and I have enjoyed your company on the few occasions I have had the pleasure of it." He paused for a moment before continuing. "I was wondering if I might perhaps call on you…at a future time…at your home," he stumbled over his words.

Catherine was surprised to find Lord Harington speaking in such an awkward and unsure manner. He always seemed so confident and sure of himself. It endeared him to her even more that the intimate conversation they had just shared.

Strangely, his faltering made Catherine feel more bold. She stopped in her tracks and faced him.

"Lord Harington, are you asking me if I might permit you to call on me," she paused just a moment before adding, "in order that you may court me?"

"I...," Brooks' eyes fell to his feet. Raising them back up to meet hers he said with confidence, "Yes, Miss Elmsworth, that is precisely my intent. That is, if you should agree to it, of course."

Catherine gave a show of great thought on the matter before answering. "I think, Lord Harington," she said, eyeing him carefully as though summing up his character, "that, as I also enjoy your company and conversation, I will allow you to call. But, I am afraid that it must be with the understanding that it is in pursuit of friendship only." She let her eyes meet his briefly. "As you may have ascertained from our recent conversation, I...that is, my heart-," she stammered.

"Say no more, my lady," Brooks intercepted, raising his palm to stop Catherine's speaking. "You need not explain further. I understand completely, and I shall be quite content to adhere to your request."

His thoughtfulness and tender acquiescence touched Catherine's heart so strongly, that she feared it might bring tears. Turning away with an abrupt "Thank you," she walked briskly toward the main gathering of the party guests. She had a sudden desire to be amongst them rather than alone in Brooks' presence.

Following quickly after Catherine, Brooks called out, "Miss Elmsworth!" As he caught up to her, he touched her arm, urging her to a halt. "Catherine," he spoke earnestly. "I must ask one more thing of you."

Keeping her eyes facing forward, she asked, "And what might that be, my lord?"

"Please, as we have been acquainted with one another for some time now and, I believe, have formed the beginning of a close friendship, I really must insist that you call me by my given name."

Catherine pondered his request for a brief moment. "Very well, my lor-, Brooks," she agreed, resuming her brisk steps.

As they joined the others, Catherine was a bit surprised to find herself smiling more and feeling more light-spirited than she had in weeks. On the carriage ride home that evening, she reflected on the time she had spent in conversation with Lord Harington...

Brooks...and she realized that she really had quite enjoyed his company. Perhaps they were to become good friends, after all.

Aunt Margaret could not have been more pleased when Catherine told her over breakfast the next morning that she should be expecting Lord Harington to come calling. She very nearly drove herself into frenzy over it. Catherine gave up trying to convince her aunt that it was not the enormous event she was making it out to be.

As for herself, the more she thought about it, the more Catherine began to question her decision to allow Brooks to call on her. It was true that she had felt a level of comfort in talking with him that she had not felt with anyone else, save Mary. But was she really ready to let him in? Did she really want him to be her friend? She was certain he wanted more from her than she was at liberty to give.

Her heart still belonged only to Garrett. He had lodged himself there firmly from the moment she had first seen him, and despite the time and distance that now separated them, Catherine could not deny that he occupied her heart still, as well as most of her thoughts. She was certain her heart would not be easily swayed to let go of him, nor did she want it to.

CHAPTER TEN

"Ah, well may we hope,
when this short life is gone,
To meet in some world of
more permanent bliss;
For a smile, or a grasp of the hand,
hastening on,
Is all we enjoy of each other in this."
from *And Doth Not A Meeting Like This*

Garrett stood before the door of his father's house, dreading what might await him on the other side of it. He had received the urgent message from his mother begging him to return home posthaste as his father was gravely ill, and it could not be determined whether or not he would survive. Garrett had quickly arranged for his departure and, thanking Lord and Lady Hawthorne for their kindness and hospitality, had boarded a coach to take him to the coast where he could catch a ferry to Dublin. Once there, rather than spend a week or more travelling by coach, he had purchased a horse, which would afford him a much quicker, if less comfortable, journey.

Along the way, when he was not nervously fretting over his father's health, Garrett's thoughts turned to the green-eyed beauty, Catherine, and the kiss they had shared. He knew she was not a wanton woman, that more than likely, she was a virgin, but there had been such abandoned passion in that kiss that just the memory of it caused a stirring within him, both in his breeches and in his heart.

He had kissed women before, a goodly number of them, truth be told, but never had one of them caused such turmoil throughout his entire body. It seemed every part of him had been affected by her. He was unable to stop his thoughts from constantly wondering back to her, even though it had been weeks since he'd last seen her.

He now held regret over the last meeting they'd had. It had been Garrett's intent the night of the masquerade to tell Catherine the truth. He wanted her to know him for who he really was, not some lowly musician, strapped of funds. Even though it appeared not to matter to Catherine who or what he was, Garrett still wanted her to see him as her peer and not someone so far beneath her as to never be considered a suitable match.

That had been his whole reason for sneaking into the ball in the first place. Then, when he had held her in his arms as they'd danced, his need to tell Catherine the truth had become even more urgent. Their meeting on the terrace had been arranged for just that purpose. He tried to tell her. Then there was that kiss…that had been quite a magnificent distraction. When she'd followed that with her confession of love, Garrett could hold back no longer. He was moments away from spilling all of his secrets to her when they'd heard voices approaching.

Not wanting to create any more tinder with which to fuel her aunt's disdain for him and wanting to protect Catherine from gossip and the *ton*'s disapproval, Garrett had quickly and quietly slipped away into the darkness. That was the last time he'd seen Catherine, the last opportunity he'd had to reveal his true self to her.

The next day, Garrett had received the letter from his mother, and now here he was, back in Ireland, probably for good, with no chance of seeing Catherine ever again. It would be best for him and all concerned to just put her out of his thoughts, but he was finding that much easier said than done.

Breathing in deeply and pulling himself up to his full height, he summoned the strength he would need for whatever lay on the other side of that door. As he reached to open it, the door was suddenly flung open by Mr. Higgins, his father's manservant.

"My lord, forgive me for the delay in answering. I was attending to Lord Brennen when I heard you arrive." He bowed low, welcoming Garrett into the Brennen family home.

Handing over his coat, hat, and gloves to Mr. Higgins, Garrett inquired, "How is Father, Higgins?" He glanced up the great stairs to the landing as if he would find the answer to his question there.

"I am afraid it is very grave, my lord. He has not stirred at all today. Lady Westbrook is quite beside herself with worry. It is good you are here."

"Yes, thank you, Mr. Higgens. I will go to her right away." With that, Garrett took the huge stairs two at a time. When he reached the door to his parents' room, he knocked lightly before entering. His mother sat on a wooden ladder backed chair pulled up close to the bed, where she held her husband's hand in both of hers. When she looked up and saw Garrett, she jumped to her feet and ran toward him.

"Oh Garrett!" she cried. "Darling, I am so glad you have come. I have been worried sick with fear." She clutched onto Garrett as soft cries emanated from between her words.

After offering comfort to his mother, Garrett held her shoulders and gently pried her away from his chest. His eyes were filled with love and sympathy as he looked down upon her. Her eyes glistened with tears as she raised them to meet his.

"Mother, what happened?" Garrett asked quietly. "What is it Father suffers from?"

"The physician says it is consumption," she sobbed. "He says there is little hope of recovery at this stage." Returning to her husband's side, she said, "He has been ill for several months, son."

"Months?" Garrett echoed, unbelieving. "Mother, why did wait so long to send for me?"

"There was nothing you could have done, Garrett. The physician was doing all he could. Then it just got to the point where nothing he did was giving your father any comfort."

"I should have been here," Garrett insisted. He knelt beside his mother's chair. Taking both of her hands in his and raising them to his lips, he kissed them. Keeping his grip on them, he gazed into his mother's eyes. "Even if nothing could have been done to help Father, I still should have been here to at least offer you some comfort, Mother."

Removing one of her hands from Garrett's, she placed it on top of his with a gentle pat. "You are here now, son, and that is all that matters."

Lord Brennen suddenly stirred, jarring both of them to attention. Garrett stood and leaned over his father's pale, shrunken body. He found it hard to reconcile the man before him with the strong, masculine man he knew as his father.

"Garrett?" His father's voice was barely above a whisper. Watery eyes tried to focus as his father looked up at him.

Garrett reached to take his father's hand in his own. It felt small and fragile. "I am here, Father," he spoke softly.

"Your mo-," Lord Brennen's words were cut short when a cough wracked his body. It was a loose, wet cough that rattled in his chest. Settled, he began once more. Garrett leaned in close to hear him.

"Take…care…mother," he said in a whisper, although it was obviously hard for him to manage even that.

Garrett felt a bit of pressure on his hand as his father tried to squeeze it.

"Good…son," he croaked, and with that he fell silent again.

Both Garrett and his mother watched with silent tears as father and husband took his last breath. Garrett's mother let out a cry and dropped her head onto the bed next to her husband. Garrett dropped his father's now lifeless hand and put his arm around his mother's shoulders. He let her cry for a time before gently leading her out of the room so that the body could be tended to. He could see his mother was exhausted. No doubt, she hadn't slept in days, not wanting to leave her husband's bedside. Garrett called for Ygrette, her mother's maid, to assist in helping her to bed.

Garrett chose to get to the library and pour himself a drink. Though he was a born and bred Irishman, he was not a drinker by nature, nor was his father, but Garrett knew the man kept a bottle of brandy in the library to offer his guests. He poured a small amount of the amber liquid into a glass and drank it down in one gulp. Setting down the glass, he glanced at his father's massive desk, spying a small stack of papers. He was certain his father would have made sure everything was in order when he'd first fallen ill, just to be safe. His father liked to be prepared.

With a heavy sigh, Garrett moved to sit on the brown, leather sofa at the opposite end of the room. He was the owner of Westbrook now. The Earl of Westbrook and Lord of the manor. His life was now laid out for him from here on out. There would be no more freedom to do as he pleased, to follow his heart and focus on his music. Now there would be an estate to run, properties to look after, his mother to take care of. Now there were responsibilities, lots of them.

CHAPTER ELEVEN

"To sigh, yet feel no pain,
To weep, yet scarce know why;
To sport an hour with Beauty's chain,
Then throw it idly by;
To kneel at many a shrine,
Yet lay the heart on none;"
from *Song from M.P.; Or
The Blue Stocking*

Lord Harington had been to call on Catherine several times since she had given him permission to do so. Catherine found she enjoyed his company more with each encounter. He was indeed the most charming man she had ever met, and handsome, to be sure. Yet, there was something more that continued to draw her to him.

She liked the fact that Brooks treated her as an equal in all things. He allowed her great freedom in expressing herself whenever they were together, as long as they were alone. When in the presence of others, particularly her Aunt Margaret, Brooks adhered strictly to the rules of society. But in private he often encouraged Catherine in pursuing her interests. He seemed to value her opinions and frequently consulted with her on all things, even those that were not generally considered womanly topics, including the economy and political goings on of London. He challenged her intellectually as no one else ever had.

For Brooks' part, he was completely smitten with Catherine. She was a beauty, that was for certain. But if one cared to look beyond her outward beauty, they would find there was much more to Miss Catherine Elmsworth. She was extremely well-read and could hold a conversation on nearly any subject. And she had ideas, many ideas, on so many different topics. She definitely was not the typical high society lady. Brooks found her to be the most fascinating woman he had ever met.

They both shared an interest in history, and visiting the local museums became a favorite pastime of theirs. They discussed every painting, every artifact, at length, ensuring that it would take many visits before they were able to see everything the museums had to offer.

Though they were frequently seen together on their outings in town or in the parks, Catherine still refused to attend social events with him. Instead, she attended all dinner parties and balls in the company of her aunt. Nor did she pay any special attention to Brooks at these affairs. Rather, she mingled as much as possible and danced with whomever asked her. She was aware there were already some rumors about that there would soon be an engagement announced between her and Lord Harington. She had no desire for that event to take place, and she wished to quash the rumors insinuating such a thing.

One afternoon Catherine sat with Brooks and Aunt Margaret in the parlor having afternoon tea.

"Lord Harington, do you enjoy the symphony?" asked Aunt Margaret. She took a dainty sip of her tea.

"I am fond of it, yes," Brooks answered, "though I have not been to the symphony yet this season. It seems there are just too many other pursuits to keep one occupied," he said, glancing covertly at Catherine. Addressing Lady Hathaway, he continued. "I speak, of course, of all the balls and dinner parties, as well as other social events."

"It does seem to be a very busy season this year, does it not?" Margaret agreed. "I feel as though I've barely had time to change into a fresh outfit and Catherine and I are off again to some gathering. I fear I am getting too old to face so much social activity."

"Nonsense, Aunt Margaret," Catherine interjected. "Why you have more stamina for those social gatherings than I do."

"Pish!" exclaimed Aunt Margaret. "These doings are more suited to you young people, Catherine, and if I have any say so in getting you engaged before the season is over, I plan to stay at home next season."

"I wish you great success in that endeavor, Lady Hathaway," replied Brooks jovially. He cast another sideways look in Catherine's direction.

"Goodness," Catherine said, "if the two of you are co-conspiring, I fear I shall have no say so in the matter." She looked back and forth between Brooks and Aunt Margaret.

"Don't look at me," said Brooks, raising both hands in the air. "I know better than to try and sway your decisions in any matter, particularly where a potential husband is concerned. If I thought I stood a chance, I would have already asked for your hand," he said, smiling.

"But of course, you have a chance, my lord," replied Aunt Margaret. "Otherwise, why are you spending so much of your time in the company of my niece?" She studied Catherine with a keen eye before turning her attention back to Brooks. "She seems quite fond of you, I'd say."

"Aunt Margaret, it seems you have forgotten that I am sitting right here," said Catherine. "Please refrain from talking about me as if I am not present."

"Very well," Margaret acquiesced. "We shall go back to speaking about the symphony. There is a performance next week. I think the two of you should go."

"I truly have no desire-," Catherine's response was cut short by Brooks.

"Why, that is a wonderful idea, Lady Hathaway." Appealing to Catherine, he added, "I would like it very much, Catherine, if you would join me for a night at the symphony. Shall we go?"

For her part, Catherine was finding it harder and harder to say no to Brooks Darling, the Earl of Harington. "Very well, I will go," she said, but not before giving her aunt a pointed stare.

The night of the performance, Catherine dressed with care. Most of the time she spent in Brooks' company, she wore her everyday dresses, but she wanted to make tonight special. She chose a deep royal blue gown with black lace trim. Aunt Margaret had loaned her a beautiful blue topaz necklace and matching earrings for the occasion.

Abby had done a magnificent job of styling Catherine's auburn locks. She was sure to cause a stir at the theater.

When Brooks came for her, he stood at the bottom of the stairs, waiting, as Catherine descended. As she reached the bottom of the staircase, she happened to look at him, and what she saw in his eyes startled her. She saw adoration, admiration, and delight. She saw the kind of look a girl wishes to see in her beau's eyes when he looks at her.

But Brooks was not her suitor. Catherine had insisted, and Brooks had agreed, they were just friends. True, she had told him that he was free to court her, but they had an understanding that it would not lead to an engagement. *Didn't they?* Catherine thought they had agreed on that matter, but now she couldn't quite recall whether they had or not. In any case, Brooks should not be looking at her the way he was looking at her. Catherine decided to ignore it.

"Lord Harington, don't you look dashing," she said with a teasing tone.

Bowing, Brooks said, "And you look gorgeous as always." He continued to stare at her for several uncomfortable moments.

"We should be going, should we not?" Catherine asked, hoping to spur him into action and away from gazing at her.

"Of course," he answered, allowing her to lead the way to the door. Abby waited near the door with a black velvet evening wrap in her hands. She helped Catherine into it. Catherine placed her hand on Brooks' waiting arm and let him lead her out.

Once they were seated in the earl's fancy evening coach and on their way to the theater, Catherine once again felt Brooks' eyes on her. With a great sigh, she exclaimed, "For pity's sake, Brooks, do quit gawking at me or I shall have to cancel this evening and have the coachman deposit me back home."

With a smirk, Brooks answered, "But Catherine, my dear, you are so lovely to look at, one cannot help but gawk like a schoolboy." Noting that Catherine truly was becoming a bit agitated, he amended, "Very well, my lady, I shall do my best to refrain from casting my eyes upon you." He smiled playfully at her, trying to lighten the mood. It worked, for Catherine was soon back to her delightfully engaging self, chattering unceasing until they reached the theater.

It had been such a long time since Catherine had been to a symphony concert, she had forgotten what an enchanting experience it could be, with all of the women dressed in such beautiful gowns and the men all looking so handsome in their finest threads.

Brooks, of course, had a box where they sat with a few of his acquaintances. Catherine was introduced to their lady companions, but she was content to listen to the conversations rather participate in them. There was a hushed excitement in the air as the curtains parted and the music began.

Having a recently acquired, deeper appreciation for music, Catherine found herself caught up in the drama and the passion of the music. It touched her in a way in never had before.

After a short intermission, a young violinist took the stage. Accompanied by the orchestra, he began to play a slow melody. It immediately brought to Catherine's mind the tune Garrett had been playing when she'd encountered him on the Lady Hawthorne's terrace. It was not the same tune, but similar enough that it jarred her heart, and the memories came suddenly, flooding through her. She was held captive by the music as images of a dark-haired, amber-eyed, violinist enveloped her.

It had been days, maybe even weeks, since she'd thought of Garrett. *Could she truly have forgotten him so soon?* Now she was assaulted with the memories of his smile, his touch, his kiss. All of it engulfed her to the point where she felt she could barely breathe.

"Catherine? Darling, are you all right?"

Catherine stared blankly at the face in front of her for a moment, before realizing who it was. It was Brooks, laying a hand on her arm and inquiring with a look of great concern.

"I...yes, I...I am fine," she stammered.

"It is just that you are crying, dearest" said Brooks. "Has something upset you?" he inquired hesitantly.

Oh dear! Catherine exclaimed silently, reaching up to wipe away the tears on her cheeks. Brooks handed her his handkerchief. As she dabbed at her cheeks, Catherine tried to regain her composure. Taking a deep breath, she forced a smile.

"I truly am fine, Brooks. I was just overcome by the music." *It was partially true, wasn't it?* "I thank you for your concern." Looking Brooks in the eye, Catherine hoped she was convincing. "It has been a lovely evening, Brooks, but if you wouldn't mind, I think I would like to go home now."

"Of course, Catherine, whatever you wish." Rising from his seat, he offered her his hand and helped her to her feet. She placed her hand on his arm and they made their way out of the theater.

They were both silent on the ride home, though Catherine could feel Brooks' eyes on her for practically the whole ride. She knew he wanted to ask her about her tearful response to the music, but he also knew Catherine well enough to know that if she wished him to know more, she would tell him.

When they reached Aunt Margaret's, Brooks exited the carriage first and reached to help Catherine descend. He held her there a moment.

"Catherine," he spoke, his voice soft and full of compassion. "Is there nothing I can do?"

Shaking her head slightly, Catherine answered, "Thank you, Brooks, as usual, you are very kind to ask, but no. I will be fine. I promise." She squeezed his arm reassuringly. "Thank you for taking me to the symphony tonight. It was wonderful." With those final words, she turned from him and entered the house. Brooks stood staring at the closed door for several minutes before he re-entered the carriage and left.

Thankfully, Aunt Margaret had long gone to sleep when Catherine arrived home. She hurried upstairs, longing for the sanctity of her room. Once there, she allowed her tears to flow freely. *What am I doing?* she asked herself. *Why can't I get this man out of my thoughts?* Catherine knew the answer. Garrett had won her heart. She knew she would never love another as she loved him, and she would never stop thinking of him.

How could she ever go to another musical performance when every violinist reminded her of one violinist, the one she held forever in her heart? And poor Brooks, he was so kind to her, so understanding about her refusal to enter into any sort of serious engagement with him. He was more than patient with her, and as much as she had tried to resist, she had grown quite fond of him.

She fell asleep without even changing out of her gown. She drifted into dreams, wondering if she would ever see Garrett again.

The next morning, she had resolved to try and find out what she could about Garrett Brennen, to somehow find out where he was, and to get in touch with him. She knew he was from Ireland, she believed the western part, but she knew little else of him. He had mentioned a professor of music he was studying under. Perhaps she could locate him to see if he knew of Garrett's whereabouts. She had to try, or she would never have any peace in the matter.

CHAPTER TWELVE

"Couldst thou look as dear as when
First I sighed for thee;
Every wish I breathed thee then,
Oh, how blissful life would be!"
from *One Dear Smile*

A month after his father's passing, Garrett had fully assumed ownership of his father's lands and holdings and all the responsibilities that entailed. All his life had been spent under the tutelage of his father in the ways and means of managing the estate, yet he still felt overwhelmed by it all. There was a huge difference between assisting his father and being the one in charge. At 22 years of age, he felt he would never be able to fill his father's shoes. As the only son and heir of Lord Westbrook's, however, he knew he must at least attempt it.

One day as Garrett sat behind his father's great oak desk in the library, sorting out his father's log books, Mr. Higgins brought in the mail. Rifling through the items, Garrett noticed a return address from his former music instructor, Professor Bennett. Opening it, after the obligatory greeting, Garrett was informed that a young lady had come around asking about him, a young lady named Catherine Elmsworth.

'Naturally,' the letter continued, 'I did not release any information to her, as I remembered that while you were here in England, you had wished to keep your identity a secret, and I, having no knowledge of this young woman nor her intentions, felt it wise to continue the discretion. I hope I have done as you would have wished, Lord Westbrook.'

Garrett placed the letter on the desk and bowed his head, running his hands through his hair. *Catherine.* He had been so busy since he'd left England, that he had scarcely had time to think of her. *What was she doing, seeking out his former teacher? Was she hoping to gain information of his whereabouts? She hadn't forgotten him, then.* Garrett's heart soared at the thought. *How would she feel, though, if she knew he had deceived her? Would her feelings for him change?*
He would find a way to return to England as soon as possible and tell her the truth. He hoped it would not be too late, and that she would be able to forgive his deception when she found out he was really the new Earl of Westbrook and not just a violinist. Perhaps it would change even her aunt's opinion of him.

During the weeks following the night of the symphony, Catherine had not seen Lord Harington. He had come to the house several times inquiring after her, but she had refused to meet with him. Aunt Margaret, having received no explanation regarding the matter, was quite disapproving of Catherine's behavior. Despite not knowing the cause of Catherine's sudden avoidance of Lord Harington, Margaret assured him it was only temporary. She hoped it was true. For all the time she had spent with Catherine in her home, raising her as if she were her own daughter, Margaret was at a loss in understanding her niece's insolent behavior.

Catherine was unable to ascertain any information from Cambridge regarding Garrett's whereabouts, other than what she already knew…that he had left rather suddenly. She still had no idea where Garrett was or how she could contact him. No one could give her any answers. It seemed a hopeless situation. She was not yet ready nor willing to give up on Garrett or the hope of ever seeing him again. Her heart would not allow it.

Since she was no longer out traipsing about with Lord Harington, her thoughts were once again consumed with Garrett. Every waking moment was filled with him. Memories of his kiss haunted Catherine. She was neither eating nor sleeping properly. She spent all her time in the garden, in her old routine of pacing about and reading Moore's poetry. She had even begun writing her own poetry, if one could call it poetry. She put her thoughts, her dreams, her passions down on paper daily. She wrote letters to Garrett even though she had no idea where to send them.

This went on for months. She had lost weight and become frail from not eating. Her dresses hung loosely about her. Her aunt had called for the physician on several occasions, but there was little he could do other than encourage Catherine to eat, which Margaret and Abby had been doing with little success. Mary and Anna Fatham had been to visit as well, but Catherine had hardly been able to rouse herself enough to converse with them. She was withering away and nothing anyone suggested or attempted seemed to make any difference.

One day, while she was out walking in the garden, Catherine rounded a hedge to find Lord Harington standing before her. Rendered temporarily speechless, she stood gawking at him.

"Catherine," he said, nodding his head in acknowledgement of her presence.

"What are you doing here, Brooks?" she asked spitefully. "I have no wish to speak to you." Catherine turned to go back the way she had come.

"Catherine, wait!" Brooks cried out with enough urgency that Catherine stopped her retreat. "You say you have no desire to speak to me, but please...at least listen to what I have to say," he begged. Catherine turned back to face him.

"Very well, what is it you wish to say, Brooks?"

Taking a step towards her, he began, "Catherine, I-"

Seeing her take a step back, he stopped. In a soft, pleading tone, he tried once more. "Catherine, I know you are hurting...and I know why," he said glancing in her direction. When she said nothing, he continued. "I know you love another, Catherine, and that your heart is broken over this man whom you may never see again."

Catherine's look of shock turned into a glare. "You know nothing, Brooks! How dare you come here and try to tell me you know my feelings! You do not know me at all!"

"I do, Catherine," he continued. "I do know you, better than you think I do. And I know your heart belongs to someone you can never have, but I am asking...no, I am begging you to consider another alternative to the one you are currently pursuing."

"What do you mean?"

"I mean, my dear Catherine, that you are slowly killing yourself, and it is my sincerest hope that you will consider me as an alternative to death."

"What are you saying, Brooks? Make yourself clear," Catherine demanded.

Brooks calmly and slowly stepped towards her. This time, she didn't back away.

"Your musician is gone, Catherine, and likely will never return."

A sob escaped Catherine before she could stop it. Tears fell in rivulets down her cheeks.

"You…don't …know that," she sputtered between sobs.

Brooks could not bear seeing her in such a state without offering some comfort. It was suddenly unimportant to him whether or not she accepted his proposal. He wanted her in his arms. He wanted to help her bear this pain. He would bear it for her if there were any way possible for him to do so.

Brooks reached out to her, his eyes full of sorrow and compassion, and Catherine did not run away as he had feared she would. She fell into him, and his arms went around her. She grasped at his coat as sobs wracked her body, and Brooks held her tightly.

He held her there for a long time until at last, her tears subsided. Wiping frantically at her face, she took the proffered handkerchief from Brooks and wiped at her face and eyes.

"You must think I am a silly chit who cries at the tiniest provocation," she said, trying to smile. "It seems you bring out the waterworks in me, my lord."

"I think nothing of the sort, Catherine. You, my girl, are anything but a chit. You have the brain of a dozen other women, and the gumption to use it as well."

"Thank you, Brooks," she said, handing him back the handkerchief. "I suppose I need that. For someone to speak to me plainly like that, I mean." Sighing, she continued, "You are right, of course. It is very likely that I will never see Mr. Brennen again...ever, and I should put such thoughts out of my head. It's just that I haven't the slightest idea how to go about it."

"Perhaps a distraction of some sort," Brooks offered innocently. "If you would allow me, I would be most willing to provide such a distraction." *Please say yes.* On the outside, Brooks maintained a casual, friendly, only slightly persistent demeanor, but on the inside, he fell at Catherine's feet begging her to comply. If only Catherine would let him, he was willing to do anything and everything within his power to make her forget her violinist.

Catherine thought for a moment. She knew she could not keep on going the way she was. Brooks was right, she was killing herself, withering away to nothing. She had only been in this world for a short nineteen years, and in that time, she had been through her share of suffering and loss. She had survived, though, through all of it, and she would certainly survive this heartache as well.

And why not let Brooks rescue her? He was a good man, handsome and charming, a wonderful conversationalist, and he treated her the way a woman should be treated, the way Catherine wanted to be treated – with respect, kindness, and admiration. If she were to release even a small part of her heart to love someone else, she could not think of anyone better than Brooks Darling to be the recipient. If she could not have Garrett, she could at least have someone she cared for and who cared greatly for her.

"I believe you are correct, Brooks, it is a distraction I need," Catherine gave her answer. She continued talking, unaware of the great relief that poured through Brooks. His body visibly relaxed and he could not keep the smile from his face. "After all, when I was going out to the galleries with you and attending the parties and such, I hardly thought of Mr. Brennen." A small smile played at her lips. "We will simply have to avoid the symphony from now on."

Chuckling at Catherine's attempt to lighten the underlying message of her comment, Brooks took both of Catherine's hands in his and held them gently in his own. "It is so good to see you smile, Catherine. You have the loveliest smile." He looked deep into her eyes.

"I truly wish nothing but joy and happiness for you, and I promise you I will do whatever I can to see that you have both." He ever so lightly placed a kiss first on her right hand, then on her left, before releasing them. "Why don't we start with something that won't be too taxing on you as you are recovering your health? I shall call for you tomorrow afternoon and we shall go for a carriage ride."

"That would be lovely, Brooks. The weather has been so nice in London of late. Perhaps we could make it a picnic," Catherine suggested.

"Yes, that is a wonderful idea!" Brooks readily agreed. "We can take a short ride to the country and spend the afternoon if you feel up to it."

Warming to the idea, Catherine thought of how nice it would be to invite Mary and Anna to come along.

"Perhaps you would like to invite a few friends to enjoy the day with us," Brooks, once again, seemed to be reading her thoughts.

"Oh yes, Brooks, what a fine idea!" She was becoming a bit giddy with the anticipation of it. "I would love to ask Mary and Anna Fatham to come along. I am afraid I treated them rather badly when they came to visit," she pouted.

"And what of their brother, Harry?" asked Brooks. "Would you care to invite him and his fiancé, Lady Covington as well?"

"Meredith…and Harry are…engaged?" How had such information skipped past Catherine's notice? *So, Meredith is the one on whom he recast his affections.*

"Yes, I would have thought you had known already, as close as you are to his sisters."

Catherine shrugged. "Well, as I said, I was not exactly the most welcoming to them when I last saw them. I think it would be great fun to invite all of them though. I shall send out the invitations right away."

As they talked, they had wandered to the front of the house where Lord Harington prepared to take his leave. Taking Catherine's hand again in his, he bowed low over it but did not place a kiss there this time.

"It has been a great pleasure to spend time with you again, Catherine. As I am sure you are aware, you were greatly missed these last few weeks."

Catherine blushed slightly at Brooks' endearing words. *He really is such a sweet man,* she told herself. And she agreed.

"You are so kind, Brooks. Thank you so much for coming today. You literally came to my rescue, and for that I am most grateful. I look forward to tomorrow."

"Till then, my lady," Brooks said with a smile and, pulling himself up into the carriage and settling himself on the seat, he tipped his hat and was off.

CHAPTER THIRTEEN

"Nights of music, nights of loving,
Lost to soon, remembered long

When we went by moonlight roving,
Hearts all love, and lips all song,"
from *Nights of Music*

The outing was a wonderful success. Harry arrived at the same moment Brooks' carriage pulled up in front of the house. He'd brought along Mary, Anna, and Meredith. Catherine had asked Mary to join her and Brooks in their carriage so that they would have a chaperone. During the ride out of town, Mary was a fount of giddiness as she informed Catherine of all the goings on about town that she had missed in the weeks she'd spent moping around.

Mother Nature was good to them and the weather remained perfect the entire afternoon. Catherine enjoyed being in the company of her friends again. She was truly happy for Harry and Meredith who seemed completely besotted with one another. There was much laughter and gaiety throughout the afternoon. Catherine was returned home a very tired, but very content young woman.

With a wave of goodbye to her friends, she dragged herself up the stairs to her room. She was exhausted and once there, she fell onto her bed without even a thought of removing her clothes first. Later, she was awakened by Abby who roused her just enough to be cooperative in the removal of her clothes. She slid her soft nightrail down over her body while Abby pulled back the covers on the bed. Catherine snuggled beneath them and soon she had fallen back into a restful sleep.

"Good morning, Catherine, dear," Aunt Margaret greeted her the next morning as she entered the breakfast room. "I must say you look well this morning, better than I've seen you look in weeks. Did you have a pleasant outing with your friends yesterday?"

Catherine served herself some eggs and toast as the maid poured her some tea. Adding a bit of cream and sugar, Catherine smiled at her aunt as she stirred. Ordinarily, Catherine liked her tea served black, but in the mornings, she always preferred it lighter and with a touch of sweetness.

"It was wonderful, Auntie. I hadn't realized how much I'd missed them all." She set her spoon on the edge of the saucer and took up her cup. After taking a small sip, she continued, "We had a splendid time of it. And the food! It was heavenly. I must remember to thank cook for the delicious taste temptations she prepared for us."

"It is certainly good to have my Catherine back again," Aunt Margaret remarked. "I was beginning to believe I had lost her for good. If I had known Lord Harington held the secret key to unlock the prison you had cast yourself in, I would have had him come sooner."

Catherine eyed her aunt warily. "You mean to say you asked Brooks to come?"

"Not at all dear," Margaret corrected. "Why, I could in no way keep that young man away as besotted as he is. He came by here every day, but I would not allow him entry. I merely meant that I would have invited him in had I known he held the power to save you from yourself."

"Hmmm...yes, I suppose I must admit that Brooks does have a certain power over me. He can be very convincing at times. And he is so level-headed, it is hard not to take his words into consideration."

She looked wistfully at nothing in particular. "I know he cares for my well-being, and that he would not tell me anything that wasn't true. He sometimes seems to know me better than I know myself."

"Perhaps if you were to give him a chance, niece, you might find that you care for him as well. I know you care for him as a friend, but if you would allow it, I am quite certain that particular friendship could grow into something more."

"What are you hinting at, Auntie?" Catherine narrowed her eyes at Margaret. "You think I should marry him, don't you? Of course, you would encourage a marriage with *Lord Harington*," Catherine's ire was up now and growing at an increasingly rapid rate. "And why not? He is handsome, and rich, and he runs in the correct social circles to suit you, does he not?"

Rising from her chair, her barely eaten breakfast ignored, Catherine placed her hands on her hips, scowling at her aunt. "Well, let me tell you, Aunt Margaret, that if I am to marry Brooks, it will not be because he is handsome, or because he has money or social standing. He is a good man, Auntie. A far better man than I have ever met, or than I deserve. He showers me with admiration, reveling in my desire to speak my own mind. He encourages me to do so, in fact. He is a true friend and a true gentleman. I am quite sure I could never find a better man for a husband."

Catherine suddenly stopped her tirade, realizing what she had just said. She was defending Brooks, a man who certainly needed no defending, to her aunt. And, she had just admitted that she could never find a better man to have as a husband. *Was that true? Is that what she truly believed? If it was true, then what was there to keep her from marrying Brooks?*

Only one thing stopped her…Garrett.

Catherine needed time to collect all the thoughts that were suddenly swimming around in her head. She needed to sort them out and make some sense of them.

"Please excuse me, Aunt Margaret," she spoke distractedly to her aunt from her daze. "I will be in the garden."

Margaret watched her niece go, a small smile playing at the corners of her mouth. She was almost certain there would be an announcement of an engagement very soon.

Catherine was shocked at the realization that she might conceivably be in love with Brooks. *Did she love him? Could she love him…enough to marry him? And what of Garrett? Could she just toss him away and marry someone else? What did that speak of her love for him? Was she really so fickle in her affections that she could forget about him so easily?*

No, she couldn't forget about Garrett...ever. He was branded on her heart and would remain there till the day she died. Brooks knew that. And yet he still wanted her, knowing he would always have to share that space in her heart with someone else. Tears fell down Catherine's face as the full knowledge of Brooks' love for her overwhelmed her. It would be so unfair of her to marry him, knowing she could never love him the way he loved her. She could never give the complete and sole devotion he lavished so abundantly on her.

And Garrett...did she even truly love him? For if she did, how could she possibly wed another? She knew the love she felt for Garrett was true. That love was so strong from the very first, that it had to be true. When Garrett touched her, she became alive. No one else's touch ignited her the way his did. And his kiss? In all her remaining days, Catherine doubted she would ever again experience a kiss like her first one with Garrett. Now it would forever be her only one with Garrett.

Brooks was right. Hadn't Catherine said as much to him? There was no certainty in life or in love, but Catherine remained fairly certain that she would never again see Garrett Brennen. He would live on as a memory, but he may as well be dead to her. If she continued to hang on to the tiny thread of hope of ever seeing him again, she would never be able to fully live her live. She would become a sullen old maid, surviving on old heartbroken memories. She had seen what that future looked like during the time she had mourned over Garrett.

It was Brooks who had saved her, Brooks who had placed in her the inclination to want to live again. She owed him her life. If she couldn't love him with her whole heart, she could at least give him the life he wanted, a life with her as his wife. Catherine knew she could be a good wife to Brooks. She cared for him greatly and wanted him to be happy. He claimed to want the same for her. Why, then, shouldn't they be that happiness for each other? In time, perhaps Catherine's feelings might improve and she might grow to truly love him. When he proposed (for she was certain he most definitely *would* propose), Catherine would say yes.

On the morning of her wedding, Catherine was a bundle of nerves. Mary, her maid of honor, and Anna, a bride's maid, had both spent the night on the eve of this special day in order that they might help Catherine prepare for the wedding. Abby had laid out Catherine's wedding gown on the bed whilst she assisted the ladies in preparing for the momentous occasion. After long, lingering soaks in the tub and helping one another style their hair, they began to dress.

The wedding gown was ivory silk with French lace at the bodice and cuffs. Tiny pink roses and silken ribbons adorned the front of the dress and the hem of the lace train. Aunt Margaret had ordered it made as soon as Catherine's engagement had been announced. No doubt, she had been planning it for some time. If it had been possible, Catherine believed her aunt would have had them wed the very next day after Brooks had proposed rather than waiting the three months till their chosen date. It had been three very hectic months, and now Catherine was ready for it to end. After today, she hoped things would settle once more.

When she stood in front of the floor-length mirror in her gown, she was overcome with emotion. She wished her father and mother could be here for this day. Moments like this were when she missed them the most, even after all this time. Her father should be the one walking her down the aisle rather than her uncle Matthew, a man she hardly knew. Being her nearest male relative, he had been called upon by his sister, Margaret, to perform the task. At least he had been agreeable to it, for that Catherine was thankful. She could think of no one else she could have asked except for her friend Harry, and that would have been awkward indeed.

Lifting a dainty handkerchief from the dressing table, she blotted away her tears. Mary came to her side, placing an arm around her shoulders. Anna joined them. As they stood together there in front of the mirror, Catherine smiled, happy that her two best friends were there to be a part of her special day.

Catherine sat as Abby put the final touches on her hair, adding strings of pearls interspersed with sprigs of baby's breath and tiny pink roses. Aunt Margaret bustled in just as they were finishing.

"You look radiant, my dear!" she exclaimed. "A vision of loveliness," she cooed, admiring her niece. "How I have waited for this day, my darling niece. I could not possibly be any happier than I am today. You will be a beautiful bride. You are marrying the most generous and kind and loving of men. I am certain the two of you shall be supremely happy together."

Pulling a small box from behind her back, Aunt Margaret went on, "Now, one last thing, my dear girl. I have something for you." She handed the box to Catherine.

"But Aunt Margaret, you have given me so much already, and I am so grateful. You don't need to give me anything else, truly you don't."

Lady Margaret answered with a voice full of emotion. "It is not from me, my dear."

"Then who?" asked Catherine curiously, taking the box from her aunt. She examined it and found no tag or note. She opened the box. Her mouth formed a small 'o' as she lifted a string of perfect pearls out of the box. Attached in the middle was a small locket. Catherine looked up at her aunt, awaiting an explanation.

"It was your mother's. Open it."

Catherine opened the locket to find two tiny paintings, one of her mother and one of her father. She couldn't speak as fresh tears flowed freely down her cheeks.

"Your father had it made for your mother and he gave it to her on their wedding day."

"Yes," Catherine's voice was a mere whisper. "I remember." She paused, taking in a deep breath. "I remember it now. Mother always wore it. She never took it off. But, how did you-?"

"How did I come to be in possession of it?" her aunt asked. "It was sent to me along with a few other small items that were among your mother's things."

"You never told me you had some of her things," Catherine said, frowning.

"I wanted to wait for a special moment like this to give it to you, Catherine." She stepped forward and, standing behind Catherine, she wrapped her arms around Catherine's shoulders in a warm hug. "As I am certain Lizzy would have. I wanted you to feel her, and your father, here with you today.

Reaching up to pat her aunt's arm around her, Catherine answered, "I do, Aunt Margaret. I do. And you are right, of course. This truly is the perfect moment for such a meaningful gift to be given." Swinging around on her small stool, she wrapped her aunt in a great, heartfelt hug, and placed a kiss upon her cheek.

"Thank you so much, Aunt Margaret, for this and for everything. You have been so wonderful to me and given me so much. I know I have not always been the easiest person to deal with, but I am forever indebted to you for all the kindness and love you have shown me."

"You have been a joy and a treasure to me in my old age, Catherine. When my dear William passed, I thought I was to spend the rest of my life alone, as we were not blessed with children of our own. But then you came to live with me, and you've brought me such happiness, my dear child. I only wish for you to know that same happiness."

They embraced for a moment more before Abby informed them they had better get things underway. It was time to head over to the church, and if they didn't leave soon, poor Lord Harington would begin to think he'd been left standing at the altar.

The ladies made haste and arrived without a moment to spare. Uncle Matthew escorted Aunt Margaret to her seat, returning to Catherine's side just as the music started. Two of Brooks' good friends from his school days stood ready to escort Mary and Anna to the front of the church. They each held out an arm to their lady and proceeded up the aisle to take their places at the front.

Uncle Matthew turned to Catherine and held out his arm to her. "Are you ready my dear?"

Catherine could not remember ever being so nervous. She remembered she had been very nervous at her very first ball, but this was different. At a ball, there is much going on all at once, and no one person is singled out for attention, but this was her day, she was to have every eye in the room on her for the duration of the ceremony. What if she should misstep, or say the wrong word? Shakily taking her uncle's arm, Catherine mustered her courage and they moved toward the aisle.

As they began their slow walk up the aisle, Catherine raised her head and looked toward the altar at the front of the church. There was Brooks, looking so handsome in his groom attire. His gaze was wholly on her as she moved closer and closer to him. Her eyes held his, and she drew strength from them. The many guests in the pews faded away, and Catherine found she wasn't nervous anymore. She didn't care what others thought, or if she might do something to cause embarrassment to herself or her loved ones.

All she cared about was this man, this wonderful man, who had come to mean so much to her, and was soon to be her husband. For a very brief moment, an image of Garrett flashed in her mind, but it was pushed away by the deep blue caverns of Brooks' eyes as they held her so lovingly in their gaze.

This is right, Catherine told herself. *I am doing the right thing. Brooks is a good man who will*

treat me well, and I am lucky he chose me to love.
She saw that love and adoration pour out and
encompass her as she met Brooks at the altar, and
her uncle released her. She took Brooks' arm and
they turned to face the vicar.

Catherine found her mind wondering as the
'dearly beloved' speech began. *True, Brooks'
touch does not ignite my skin as Garrett's did,
but that may come as we become better
acquainted with each other as man and wife. I
believe he is a man of passion.* With that thought,
Catherine realized that she and Brooks had never
actually kissed. Even when he had proposed and
she'd accepted, he gave her only a slight kiss on
the cheek. Catherine thought he was only
adhering to some strict gentlemanly rule he had
regarding kissing young women he was not
married to, but perhaps there was more to it.

She began to worry about what it might be like
for them in the bedchamber. *What an alarming
thing to be thinking about in the middle of your
wedding!* she chastised herself. *Goodness, girl,
get a hold of yourself. You are getting married,
the least you could do is pay attention and keep
your thoughts from going astray.* She turned her
head slightly to find Brooks watching her, a look
of puzzlement furrowing his brow. She returned
her focus to the vicar and the words he was
saying.

"Do you, Miss Catherine Marie Elmsworth, take Lord Brooks Byron Darling, The Earl of Harington, to be your husband…?"

In a dizzy blur, Catherine repeated the words as the vicar instructed. She vaguely heard Brooks do the same. Before she knew it, the ceremony was over, and Brooks was giving her a chaste kiss to seal the deal. They were husband and wife. She was now Lady Catherine Darling, The Countess of Harington.

After the ceremony ended, all the attendees were invited back to Aunt Margaret's where a fantastic wedding feast had been prepared for all to enjoy. The festivities went on for hours. There was much dancing, eating, and general gaiety. By the time it was all over, Catherine was exhausted as Brooks helped her into the carriage that would take her to her new home.

All of Catherine's possessions had been moved into Brooks' home just days before, all except for the trunks that had been packed for their 2-month long honeymoon trip to Paris. Brooks had planned everything in advance for the trip that would begin the very next day.

By the time they arrived at the home they would now be sharing, Catherine had fallen fast asleep in the coach. Not wanting to wake her, Brooks removed her from the carriage as gently as he could and carried up the stairs to bed. He laid her on the bed and with a bit of struggling and maneuvering, he managed to remove her from her wedding gown and various undergarments which bound her.

Catherine roused herself. Her heavy eyelids barely opened as she spoke. "Brooks?" she asked wearily.

"Shh, darling," Brooks hushed her. "We are home, love. Go back to sleep."

"But…our wedding night," she mumbled sleepily.

"Don't worry about that," said Brooks with a gentle smile. "We'll have plenty of time for that on our honeymoon." Leaving her in her chemise, he pulled back the covers on the bed. "Now snuggle in here and go to sleep, my love."

Catherine did as he ordered and crawled under the blankets. Brooks pulled them up around her, and she was soon sound asleep. Brooks gazed lovingly at his new bride. With a light caress, he brushed a strand of hair from her face, his fingertips relishing the softness of her skin. Bending over her, his lips lightly touched her forehead in a gentle kiss. Watching her for a moment more, he then retreated to his own room across the hall.

He hadn't wanted to presume Catherine would share his room, so he had given her rooms of her own, just across the hall from his. He hoped, of course, that she *would* choose to share his, but even if she did, Brooks wanted her to have a place all her own, a space she could retreat to whenever she so desired. He knew she often preferred to be alone.

Catherine awoke to the stirrings of her maid, Abby, stoking a fire in the fireplace to ward off the chill of the morning. Worried that she may have slept too late in the morning and thus delayed the honeymoon departure, Catherine sprang up in her bed. "Goodness, Abby, what time is it? Have I overslept?"

Abby turned around to face Catherine, "Not at all, *Lady Harington*," she replied with a grin. "You've plenty of time to dress and have a bite before it's time for us to go." Abby, along with Brooks' man, Charles, would be accompanying the couple on their trip to France. "I have your bath ready, my lady, and your traveling dress is laid out.

Rising from the bed, Catherine noticed she was dressed only in her chemise. "Abby, did you help me undress last night?"

"No, my lady, that bit would have been done by your husband." She turned slightly away, a sly smile on her face.

Catherine frowned as memories from the previous night flooded her thoughts, memories of the wedding and dancing with Brooks at the reception. She remembered leaving the reception, but not arriving home. Her face grew warm as she remembered Brooks removing her gown and putting her to bed. She put her face in her hands, overcome with embarrassment. *Oh dear! What sort of woman falls asleep on her wedding night? And barely stirs even as her new husband undresses her?*

Shaking her head back and forth whilst still holding it, her auburn locks falling over her shoulder, she chastised herself. *What must Brooks think of the woman he married? That she is a clueless dunderhead who hasn't a clue what should take place between a man and his new wife on their wedding night,* she answered herself. How could she ever face him this morning?

Catherine entered the breakfast room overcome with mortification and embarrassment. As soon as Brooks saw her, he rose, setting his newsprint on the table next to his plate.

"Catherine, my darling, you look wonderfully refreshed this morning," he smiled, taking her hands in his and brushing a light kiss upon her cheek. "You were quite depleted by the time we left the reception last night. I trust you slept well?" He pulled out the chair to the right of his and held her hand as she seated herself. Returning to his own seat, he waited for her answer.

Words did not immediately come to Catherine. What could she possibly say? She had determined long before she and Brooks had become engaged that there should always be honesty between them. Catherine believed it was the best basis for a good relationship, and Brooks had agreed. She stared at the empty plate in front of her, unable to meet his gaze.

Clearing his throat, Brooks inquired of her, "Was the bed not to your liking?" Something must have disagreed with her. *Why wasn't she speaking to him this morning? Surely, he hadn't done anything to get her ire up so early into their marriage. Why, they had yet to even begin their honeymoon.*

Catherine lifted her head and met Brooks' warm, questioning eyes. She may as well get it over with. *Here goes,* her thoughts pushed her forward.

"Brooks, I…I am so ashamed," she stammered. "I feel like a complete ninny for falling asleep last night. On our wedding night!" She cried. "You must be thinking such awful things toward me this morning. I am truly so very sorry."

"What are you going on about, Catherine?" he hushed her. Taking her hand in his once more, Brooks first kissed it, then rubbed his own hand reassuringly over it. "I most certainly am not thinking anything of the sort, my darling. Why ever would you say such a thing?"

Choking out her tearful reply, Catherine answered, "It was *our wedding night,* Brooks, and I fell asleep! You must think me such a bore of a wife." Grasping his hand in earnest, she pledged, "I promise you, I will make it up to you. You will see I am not a cold fish in the bedroom, nor am I afraid to fulfill my wifely duties."

Throwing back his head with a loud chuckle, Brooks exclaimed, "A cold fish? You? Catherine, my love, you could never be a cold, or boring, anything." He patted her hand once more before picking up his fork to resume his meal. "I knew how very tired you were, dearest, and I had no intention of forcing myself upon you while you were in such a state. As I told you last night, there will be plenty of time for that on our honeymoon." He flashed Catherine a devilish grin before taking a bite of his breakfast.

Her cheeks ablaze, Catherine spooned eggs and sausage onto her plate. Reaching for her tea cup, she raised it to her lips, peeking over the rim at Brooks. He winked at her. She nearly spilt her tea as she set it back on the saucer.

A few seconds passed in silence. Suddenly Catherine burst out laughing. When Brooks joined in, they both laughed all the more.

"I was so embarrassed," Catherine choked out between giggles, "when I woke this morning and realized what I'd done." She covered her wide grin daintily with her hand.

Brooks, relishing his wife's adorable laugh and pinked cheeks, played along. "You should have seen your face when you entered the room," he teased. "I thought *I* had done something to garner such a look."

As their laughter subsided and they were able to finish breaking their fast, Brooks finished with a final drink of his tea. He stood, stepping around the corner of the table to Catherine's side. He placed a kiss on her cheek, and nuzzling her neck, he whispered, "I was not joking, love, about the honeymoon. I plan to devour you." With those words lingering, he left the room.

A shiver ran through Catherine as his breath tickled her ear, even as her cheeks burned once more, and a stirring commenced in her womanly parts. Catherine was surprised at her body's response. Never before had Brooks' words, his touch, or even his kisses, elicited such a response.

She was reminded once again of someone who *did* stir those responses within her core. She quickly pushed Garrett from her thoughts, though, as she went to see to the final preparations for the trip to Paris.

CHAPTER FOURTEEN

"May the new ties that bind thee
Far sweeter, happier prove,
Nor ever of me remind thee,
But by their truth and love.
Think how, asleep or waking,
Thy image haunts me yet;
But, how this heart is breaking,
For thy own peace forget."
from *Fear Not That, While Around Thee*

It was early autumn when Garrett stepped out of his family carriage in front of the home of Lord and Lady Hawthorne. It had taken him several months to see to his father's burial and all of the final paperwork regarding the bequeathing of the Westbrook estate to Garrett. His mother had a very difficult time of it in the beginning, learning how to live without her husband. It helped that Garrett was there. He hated to think what she would have done had he not arrived when he did. She was doing better now, and her sister, Garrett's Aunt Rina, had arrived just a week ago for a month long stay, so the new Dowager of Westbrook would have some company while her son was away in London.

The air was crisp but, thankfully, there hadn't been much rain the past week as Garrett was travelling. The journey would have been quite unpleasant had the roads been burdened with rain. As it was, Garrett had been able to make good time on his journey. He had planned on staying at one of the better inns during this visit to London, but Lord and Lady Hawthorne had insisted he come and stay with them as before.

Just as well, as he had missed their company and hospitality, and he would also be able to find out how Catherine was faring much quicker, for he was certain Lady Hawthorne would be sure to catch him up on all the latest happenings about town. He hoped that would include news of Catherine.

Catherine's lovely face, with her emerald eyes and ginger locks, filled his thoughts as he disembarked from the carriage. How he longed to see her once again. Even as he had been busily working at the estate's management, she had never been far from his thoughts. Each and every night, no matter how tired he was, he prayed for her before he fell asleep. He prayed for her safety and well-being, wished for her great happiness, and hoped he would soon be able to hold her in his arms again. Her kiss was the last thing he thought of each night.

Later, as they dined, Lady Hawthorne chattered ceaselessly about London's high society and all of the fabulous balls and events he had missed while he was away at home. Garrett and Lord Hawthorne indulged her and spoke of little else throughout the meal. They were able to discuss their manly topics as they shared a glass of port after the meal.

Reconnoitering in the parlor, Lady Hawthorne spoke of more personal happenings among the town's elite – who had become engaged, who had added new babies to the family, etc. She still had not mentioned Catherine.

Desperate for news of his lady love, Garrett (trying to sound as nonchalant as he could) prodded, "And what news of Miss Elmsworth? If I am not mistaken, you are well acquainted with her and her aunt, are you not?"

"Oh yes, we are very well acquainted," Lady Hawthorne proclaimed. "Lady Hathaway and I are old friends. Her dear niece is away in Paris just now."

"Paris?" inquired Garrett, hoping she would elaborate a bit more.

"Oh, yes!" she exclaimed. "Well, surely you heard of Miss Elmsworth's engagement," she said. "Oh, silly me, of course you didn't all the way over there in Ireland," she giggled. Garrett tried to school his features and remain calm upon hearing the news of Catherine's engagement. "Of course, she in no longer Miss Elmsworth, but is now The Countess of Harington, having only recently married The Earl of Harington. Perhaps you remember him from your previous stay with us," she rattled on, completely unaware that Garrett's heart was breaking into a million pieces.

Married? Catherine is married? He had heard the words, true enough, but his mind would not accept them, nor would his heart. He could not bear to hear more, so he excused himself as quickly and as politely as he could, feigning fatigue from his long hours on the road.

"Oh, of course, dear boy," Lady Hawthorne granted, "you surely must be exhausted. Forgive me for prattling on so when you are so badly in need of rest. We shall see you in the morning."

"Goodnight to you both, then," Garrett said with a nod to each of his hosts, before making a hasty departure to his room.

Once there, he collapsed into the winged back chair in front of the fireplace. Bending at the waist and placing his head in his hands, he heard Lady Hawthorne's words once again. 'Catherine's engagement… Countess

Harington…recently wed.' Garrett willed himself not to let the tears fall that so precariously clung to his lashes, threatening to spill forth. *I thought we were matched in our feelings for one another,* he silently bemoaned. *If that were true, how could she marry another?*

Memories assailed him…memories of each sweet moment spent in Catherine's presence. He remembered the light springing forth from her emerald eyes when he'd first looked into them. He remembered each treasured conversation, each tender touch sending sparks of fire through his entire being. And her kiss…that moment when he knew…he *knew* he loved her. He had believed with all his heart that she felt the same for him, but now, now he knew she did not. She could not. Not if she was married to someone else.

Garrett passed the night in agony, his heart aching, his spirit broken. *Why had he come back to London? Just to suffer more than he had already? Wasn't losing his father enough? Must he also lose the woman he loved?* It was too much for him to bear.

After a near sleepless night, he informed the Marquess and Marchioness the next morning that his plans had changed, and he wouldn't be staying in town after all. They were surprised at his leaving so soon after he had arrived and, of course, would miss his company, but they were very understanding and wished him a safe journey home.

The ride back home seemed an eternity. The anxious anticipation he had brought with him on the ride to London had given way to a bitter moodiness. It accompanied him the entire trip and clung to him even after he returned home. His shortness with the house staff and the stable hands ensured they all took pains to stay out of his path and in his good favor lest they receive a good dressing down.

What little patience he retained was reserved for his mother, with whom he was always the most tender and gentle. He was a devoted son and did whatever he could to ensure her happiness. If only he could do the same for himself.

CHAPTER FIFTEEN

"Oh! No-not even when first we loved,
Wert thou as dear as now thou art;
Thy beauty then my senses moved,
But now thy virtues bind my heart."
from *Oh! No – Not E'en When
We First Met Cashmerian Air*

By the time the new Earl and Countess Harington arrived in France, Catherine had become quite enamored of her new husband. Brooks certainly knew how to treat a woman that was for certain. He was a most attentive husband, anticipating her needs and desires before Catherine herself even knew of them, and seeing to it that they were fulfilled immediately. Catherine lacked for nothing, neither in the way of physical comforts nor emotional support. Brooks was steadfast in his devotion to her, and Catherine could not help but be thankful for the blessing of such a good and kind husband. She found herself caring more for him with each passing day.

The first night of their trip was spent aboard the train in tiny, cramped quarters. They had shared a quiet candlelight dinner in a private dining car Brooks had secured for them. Over dinner and champagne, Brooks regaled Catherine with stories of his previous trips to France. Having never been there herself, Catherine had only read about the beautiful country and its history in books. Her husband told her of all the wondrous sights he would take her to see, the many beautiful cathedrals, and the museums, including the Musee du Louvre. Catherine's anticipation and excitement mounted with each tale.

After dinner they had returned to their sleeping car which barely had room enough for them both and the small traveling cases they carried with them while the rest of their luggage was stored elsewhere on the train. Catherine was trying to figure out how they would manage when Brooks slipped up behind her and embracing her, began placing soft kisses upon the nape of her neck.

His warm breath tickled, and Catherine shuddered. A moment later, a wonderful warmth began to spread through her. It began at her core, sending little streams of fire throughout her body. Turning to face her husband, Catherine put her arms around his neck and drew him closer. His lips touched hers lightly at first, tentatively, then deepening the kiss, he pulled her tightly to him.

Their bodies pressed together tightly as their lips sought to devour one another. There was a soft moan, and Catherine wasn't sure if it came from her or Brooks…or perhaps both. All she knew at that moment was that she wanted him…wanted his kiss…wanted him to touch her in ways she had never been touched.

Brooks pushed away from her and Catherine felt the sudden lack of warmth where his body had been pressed to hers. She looked at him, a question in her eyes. Had she done something wrong? Was her kiss so terrible that her new husband wanted no more from her?

A small gasp escaped her when Brooks began to unfasten her gown. She stood still as he loosened the dress and then her stays. When he placed his warm hand on her breast it was all she could do to keep from crying out. His touch was like fire on her skin and she wanted to feel that fire everywhere. When her chemise fell to the ground and Brooks bent to kiss her breast, she nearly exploded.

Never had she imagined a man's touch could make her body respond in such ways. No wonder ladies were taught to keep themselves pure until they were wed. If ever a young woman were to experience this before marriage, she would most assuredly desire to indulge in such pleasure on a regular basis. Never had she dreamed such delights awaited her in the marriage bed.

In the morning, Catherine woke to the warmth of Brooks' body snuggled up against her back, his arm draped over her possessively. She lingered there in his caress, unwilling to disturb his slumber. Both had slept in much later than was usual for them. They had not slept much the night before. Once it had begun, their delayed wedding night progressed into such bliss that Catherine could not imagine anything that could surpass it. She felt herself blushing as she recalled the many things Brooks had done to her body, each more pleasurable than the one before. This honeymoon trip was going to be the trip of a lifetime in more ways than one.

Brooks stirred and nuzzled against Catherine, emitting a contented sigh. Turning to face him, Catherine met his sleepy, hooded eyes. She took in his unshaven stubble, his tousled blonde locks, and his naked chest deciding that she quite liked this version of Brooks, so different from the prim and proper bearing he most often presented. She would have to make sure she encountered this Brooks as often as she could.

"Did I rouse you, my darling?" Catherine whispered, snuggling closer to her husband.

Cocking one eyebrow at her, Brooks grinned lazily at her. "I am most definitely aroused," he answered eagerly, wrapping his arms tighter around her and pulling her against him.

Catherine immediately felt his arousal growing between them. She giggled, "Yes...I can see that!"

"And what, my dear wife," he asked, kissing the tip of her nose, "do you propose we do about it?"

"Hmmm, let me think about it for a moment," Catherine teased.

"No thinking!" Brooks exclaimed, rising up on his elbow to get a better look at her. "We must act immediately." Lowering his lips to hers, he kissed her passionately as his hands sought her body. Catherine was more than ready for him and returned his kisses eagerly, inviting him to continue.

Later, both having been sated carnally, they washed, dressed, and sought food to fulfill their other appetite. They chatted in an easy manner while breaking their fast. Catherine marveled at her good fortune in finding a man who was a true friend as well as a lover, someone she could easily converse with, and one whose company she readily enjoyed. She had heard tales of women who had landed in unhappy marriages with overbearing, sometimes even abusive, men, men who had many adulterous relationships with mistresses without giving a single care to their wives. Catherine considered herself very lucky, indeed.

As their time in Paris drew to an end, Catherine found herself fantasizing about what her life would be like when they returned home. The first two months of her marriage spent in such a wonderful place seemed a bit ethereal, like a dream she would soon have to wake from. She imagined things would be much different once Brooks had returned to his regular duties of managing his estates and his money, and she was left to her own devices for entertainment during the hours he was either working in his office or out and about in town attending meetings and what not.

Being the wife of such a prominent man, Catherine would be expected to host dinners and balls on a somewhat regular basis. While she had attended many of these types of gatherings, she had never hosted anything, other than the dinner she and Aunt Margaret had hosted for Lord and Lady Mosbey and their family, months ago. That would certainly be an undertaking. When the time came, she would have to consult with someone, perhaps Lady Mosbey or Lady Hawthorne, on how to go about hosting a large event.

All of the packing for the trip home had been completed, and they were set to leave for London the next morning. Brooks had ordered room service to bring a romantic dinner for two up to their room. For two months, they had been roaming all over Paris from morning till evening, taking in everything there was to see. On this, their last night in the city of love, he just wanted to relax and spend a quiet evening with his beautiful wife.

They woke bright and early the next morning, both suddenly anxious to be on their way home. Though their time together in Paris had been thrilling, they were worn out from all the activity, both the daytime excursions and the nighttime activities. Catherine longed for some quiet time to herself, enjoying Brooks' immense library or the beautiful gardens at his family estate, Harington House.

Soon, she knew she would have to begin playing the good, entertaining wife. Brooks was very well-known and held in high regard amongst society and, being so, he was invited to (and expected to attend) many social gatherings. Unfortunately for Catherine, she had not considered what her part would be in that scenario before she had accepted Brooks' proposal. Not that she wasn't committed to being and doing whatever was required in order to support her husband's standing within the ranks of high society.

These thoughts weighed on her as they finally neared their destination. Brooks had decided they would go directly to Harington upon their return, for the London season was nearly at an end. He thought it would be easier on Catherine, adjusting to her new position as lady of the house with a smaller staff and a gentler schedule to maintain. Catherine was ever grateful she had such a kind and thoughtful husband. They would both be able to be a little more relaxed here in the country than they would be in the city.

The last leg of their journey, riding from London by carriage, seemed the most daunting. Rain descended upon them the moment they'd exited the train. Luckily, Brooks' driver was there waiting for them and they were quickly settled inside the carriage and on their way. The torrents had pelted the vehicle the entire way. The roads had become small rivers in many places and fording them was quite treacherous, as the sheets of rain were blinding, making it all the more difficult to be able to see the road ahead.

Catherine pitied the poor driver and footman as they endured the entire trip soaking wet. She would offer them both some time to thaw out by the fire and a cup of hot cocoa when they arrived home.

CHAPTER SIXTEEN

"So brief our existence, a glimpse, at the most,
Is all we can have of the few we hold dear;
And oft even joy is unheeded and lost,
For want of some heart,
that could echo it near."
from *And Doth Not A Meeting Like This*

They were two miles from reaching Harington House when the carriage hit a deep rut in the road. As the carriage began to tip, Brooks threw himself toward the downward side of the carriage wall in an effort to soften Catherine's fall. Just as he landed hard against the inside wall, the carriage door became unlatched. The force of gravity pulled Brooks through the open door. He clung to the doorframe with all his strength, but he could not keep hold. Realizing his fate, he turned sad, scared, loving eyes to Catherine and suddenly he was gone.

Catherine grabbed for Brooks as the careening carriage landed hard on its side upon the solid earth, but it was too late. He had disappeared through the carriage door just as the chassis landed with a loud crash. Catherine's head hit hard on the solid frame and her body went limp as she landed in a heap.

There were faint voices and sounds of scurrying when Catherine regained consciousness. A minute could have passed or an hour, she knew not which. She lay twisted up in what was once the top corner of the carriage, now balanced at a precarious angle on its side. A sharp pain pierced her head as she tried to move. Her eyes searched the enclosure for Brooks, but he was not there. The horrible vision of him falling through the open door slammed into her thoughts. Lifting her hand to her head, she moaned, and all went black again.

"My Lady...Lady Harington...Countess, can you hear me?"

A voice pierced the haziness as Catherine tried to open her eyes...a man's voice. *Brooks?* She struggled to open her eyes. "Brooks?"

"No, my lady, it is Carson, the footman."

Catherine moved her limbs, trying to raise herself. The pain in her head was like a knife being thrust through it.

"Lie still, my lady. Thomas has gone for help."

"Brooks," she murmured, trying again to raise herself. She glanced around at the surroundings. She was no longer in the carriage. She felt the ground, hard and wet, beneath her. She lay beneath a large tree, which provided her some shelter from the still pouring rain.

She looked across the road to where the carriage lay on its side. Her eyes halted and she drew in a sharp breath when she saw Brooks' body lying several yards away from her. He was pinned under the fallen carriage, his body from the waist down, hidden beneath the rig.

"Brooks!" Despite the intense pain, Catherine hauled herself up and, with Carson's help, made her way to her husband. Falling to the ground next to him, Catherine took his head in her lap. A sob escaped as she gently stroked his mud matted hair.

She gasped when his eyes suddenly opened. "Brooks! Oh, my darling, Brooks, you're alive!" She held him to her tightly. Releasing his body slightly so she could see his face, Catherine realized he was trying to speak. The rain began to fall harder and was so loud, she could barely hear his words.

"I...love...you...Catherine," he whispered. "From...first...moment...I...saw...you."

"I love you, too, Brooks," cried Catherine, and at that moment, with all her heart, she knew it was true. She did love Brooks. She wasn't sure when or how it had happened, but she did truly love him, with every part of her being.

"Time…," Brooks was barely breathing as he forced the words out, "we had…was…good."

Tears flowing down her face, blending with the rain, Catherine nodded.

"Yes, my darling, it was more than good. It was wonderful…a most glorious time, and we shall have many more happy times together, my love."

"I…lo-," Brooks' voice faltered on his words. He blinked his eyes as he tried to focus on his wife's face, her rain-soaked hair, and tear-leaden, mossy eyes fading from view as he slipped away.

Catherine watched wordlessly as Brooks' eyes glazed over, the life draining out of them. She held him tightly to her breast. A loud cry rent the sodden silence of the countryside. Catherine was startled to realize it had come from her. Sobbing, she clung to her husband's now lifeless body and the torrent washed over her. A flash of lightening pierced the sky as overwhelming ache pierced Catherine's heart to the core.

She held onto Brooks, rocking him gently, her tears falling ceaselessly, until Thomas arrived with the wagon, and strong hands on either side of her gently pried her from her grip on her husband's limp body. Blindly, Catherine let herself be led to the wagon where she was hoisted up into the bed and covered with blankets.

Taking great care, the men then lifted Brooks into the wagon, placing him next to Catherine. She turned toward her him and lifted his head, placing it once again in her lap. For the duration of the ride home, she sat staring into nothingness as she softly stroked the side of her beautiful, young, dead husband's face.

When the wagon finally stopped in front of Harington House, Catherine sat shivering in the rain, until some moments later, she was coaxed from the wagon and away from her husband's lifeless body. Abby was there at her side, guiding her upstairs to her rooms where a great fire roared. Abby helped Catherine out of her wet clothes and put her into bed.

The days passed in a blur. Catherine was kept abed for several days under the physician's orders. She had suffered a severe concussion from the accident and was badly bruised, but no other physical damage had been done to her. Emotional damage, though, that was something else altogether. Every time she woke, she remembered. Every time she remembered, fresh tears came with the memory of her dear Brooks and the last moment they had shared...that moment when Catherine had realized how much she truly loved him.

Catherine had no memory of what had transpired after that moment. Apparently, Thomas had returned with a wagon and three of the stable hands. They had been able to lift the carriage enough to remove Brooks' broken body from beneath it and place him in the back of the wagon to bring him home.

Dr. Bertrand had been waiting when they arrived at the house. Upon examining the egg-sized bump on Catherine's head, and her bruised body, the doctor had ordered a hot bath, a cup of hot tea laced with a few drops of laudanum, and complete bedrest for several days. Abby was at Catherine's side to make sure it was all accomplished. After the warm soak and the tea, Catherine had collapsed into a fatigue and opiate-induced sleep, which was much needed if her body was to heal.

Abby remained at her ladyship's bedside, keeping Catherine sedated with doses of the laudanum whenever she tried to leave the bed in search of Brooks. She knew, of course, that her husband had not survived the accident, but upon each awakening, she would call out to him, seeking him, until the memories assaulted her anew. Poor Abby was at a loss as to how to help her mistress in her distress. She just kept on as the Dr. had ordered, feeding her bowls of broth and cups of tea, laced with the laudanum.

On the fourth day after the accident, Dr. Bertrand had allowed Catherine to get out of bed for short periods, though each time she woke with remembrance of what had happened, she wished only to be returned to the cushioned oblivion provided by the laudanum. She begged more from the good doctor, claiming she was suffering from severe headaches. He willingly obliged her.

Six days after the accident, Catherine's Aunt Margaret arrived. Finding her niece in a drugged stupor, she took charge of the situation immediately. First, she disposed of the laudanum. Catherine cried for her aunt to reconsider, claiming that she was in considerable pain on a daily basis.

Having lost her own loving husband years before, Lady Hathaway was well aware of the pain Catherine suffered. She also knew that though the laudanum might mask the pain, it would not help in the healing of her niece's heart. Catherine begged, but her aunt would not relent. Instead, she gave her cups of hot tea with toast, and bowls of hot soup. She had asked the cook to add some meat and vegetables to the weak broth, hoping it would help Catherine regain her strength. Margaret offered her niece a shoulder to cry on and arms to comfort, along with a few strong words of encouragement thrown in here and there for good measure.

One week after the accident, on the day of Brooks' funeral, Catherine remained a bit bleary-eyed but thanks to her aunt's ministrations, she was at least clear-headed enough to attend her husband's funeral service.

Catherine stood rigid and solemn next to her aunt. Abby held onto her firmly on her other side. They stood together at the gravesite as the rector read from the scriptures and prayed. The service at the church had been brief. Though Brooks had many friends and acquaintances in London, his death had been so unexpected, and the funeral so soon after, that many of them had not been able to arrange their affairs in order to make the trip out to the country for the funeral.

Most of the people who had attended the service had been long-time friends of his parents who had been visiting their own country estates nearby and had heard of the tragedy. The house staff had all come to pay their respects, then dutifully rushed back to the manor to prepare for the open house reception that would follow the burial.

The only friends of Catherine and Lady Hathaway who had been able to come were Lord and Lady Mosbey along with their daughters, Mary and Anna. Their son, Harry, was not with them as he had recently married in Catherine's absence and was now on his own honeymoon with his new wife, the former Lady Meredith Covington.

As the casket was lowered into the ground, Catherine heard a soft sob behind her and knew that it would be Mary. Her dearest friend was the emotional sort and Catherine knew that Mary's heart ached for her almost as much as Catherine's own heart ached. Catherine herself had not shed a single tear throughout the service and the burial. She had cried so many tears in the past week she believed it was entirely possible she would never cry again.

As soon as they returned home, Catherine retreated once again to her room. She was still weak, and too emotionally shattered to attend to the after-funeral guests. At least that is what she claimed. In reality, she could not bear the thought of having to sit through the trivial conversations of her highborn neighbors in the wake of her distress.

She was sure they all would have endless stories to share of a Brooks she had never known, the boy, the young man, the son. Now he would forever remain in her memory the way she knew him, as Brooks the friend, the lover, the husband.

Catherine lay staring at the ceiling when there was a soft knock upon her bedroom door. She chose not to respond hoping whoever it was would just go away.

"Catherine?" It was Mary. Opening the door just a crack, she queried, "May I come in, dearest?"

Barely turning her head in the direction of the door, Catherine answered, "Of course, Mary. You are always welcome. Please, do come in."

Mustering all her energy, and with considerable effort, Catherine managed pull herself into a sitting position. Mary hurried to her side and gathered up the pillows, placing them at Catherine's back.

"Thank you, Mary," Catherine mumbled in response to her friend's caring gesture. Resting comfortably once more, Catherine closed her eyes as a heavy sigh escaped her lips.

Seating herself in the bedside chair, Mary took her friend's limp hand gently in her own. "Is there anything I can do to help ease your pain, Catherine?"

Opening one eye, Catherine answered wryly, "You can bring me more laudanum."

"I am afraid your aunt has already expressly forbidden anyone from doing just that, my friend, and with good reason, I should say. You do yourself no favors by partaking freely of that poison."

"It eases the pain," Catherine cried weakly.

"It numbs it, you mean, along with all your senses, and other bodily function. Your body begins to shut down if you have too much of it. And the Good Lord only knows what long-term effects it has on the brain."

"Hrumph," Catherine spat out, sounding remarkably like her Aunt Margaret. "Where have you heard such nonsense, Mary?"

"Why, in books, of course," her friend replied. "I have read there have been studies done on the effects of long term opiate use and the damage it does to one's body and mind. I must say, Catherine, as the voracious reader that I know you to be, I am surprised you have not read of it yourself."

Ignoring her friend, Catherine turned onto her side, facing the wall, and went back to sleep.

CHAPTER SEVENTEEN

"Oh, Memory, how coldly
Thou paintest joy gone by;
Like rainbows, thy pictures
But mournfully shine and die."
from *Song from Evenings In Greece*

Catherine was called to the London office of her husband's solicitor for the reading of his will and the dispersing of his property. As she and her husband had no children, and enough time had passed for her to know she was not carrying his child, the title and all entailed property would go to his nephew, the son of his younger brother, and Brooks' only living male relative.

Catherine would receive her bride settlement, as well as, she was surprised to learn, another 5,000 pounds per year. She was further surprised to learn that her husband had willed the London house, which was not part of the entailment, to her, as well as the libraries and any other personal belongings she desired from both houses.

Her husband's nephew, the new Lord Harington, brought no argument against this bequeathment, as he and his uncle had already discussed it before Catherine and Brooks had married, and the Earl had made it quite clear what his wishes were.

Having gone through her husband's private rooms at Harington House, Catherine had chosen a few small mementos from among her husband's personal items to keep, a pocket watch that had belonged to his grandfather, a golden locket that was his mother's, and a small volume of Byron's poetry she found on his nightstand.

She made her way to the library. She would love to be able keep the entire library, but the thought of moving all those books was quite daunting. And where would she put them? The London house already had its own full library. Catherine supposed she could store them, but what would be the purpose of keeping them if they would not be read? She decided she would choose some of her favorites to keep and donate the rest of them.

Sighing heavily as she surveyed the beautiful, dark walnut, heavy-laden shelves, she turned toward her husband's huge desk at one end of the room. There was a stack of papers there. Catherine seated herself in the heavy leather chair and took the first paper from the stack. It was a letter from the proprietor of the inn where they had stayed while in Paris, confirming their reservation for the past two months. Wiping away her sudden tears, Catherine fingered another document from the stack.

"Oh, Brooks," Catherine cried, burying her tear-streaked face in her palms, "what am I to do? *How will I ever know happiness again when such sadness has found me and taken hold of me? In my short life, I have already loved and lost two very dear men. How can I ever love again?"* She had no answers.

She could take no more of this today. Gathering up the papers she had removed from the pile, she reached to place them back on the stack when she noticed the closed file now resting on the top of the pile. It was labeled "Private" and was bound with a strap of leather. Curious, Catherine picked it up. Unwinding the leather strap, she hesitated momentarily, wondering if she should just leave it be. She debated with her conscience. Finally, she maintained that whatever information the file held, she had a right to know what was therein. She opened the file with caution, a worried frown creasing her forehead over what it might contain

A name pounced out at her. Garrett Brennen. *What on earth? Why would Brooks have anything with Garrett's name on it in his possession?* Setting the bulk of the pages down on the desk, Catherine reached for the one bearing Garrett's name.

The heading at the top of the page stated that the missive was from a Mr. Stirling's office and that this Mr. Stirling was a private investigator of some sort. Catherine could not fathom why such a document should be among her husband's papers. As she read through the page, her hands began to shake. It appeared that Brooks had hired this man, Mr. Stirling, to find out information for him on Mr. Garrett Brennen. Catherine's eyes went back to the stack of papers. Picking up another, she read that Mr. Stirling had found out where this Mr. Brennen was from and who his family was.

Garrett Brennen, The Viscount of Rathburn, was the eldest and only surviving son of Lord Patrick Brennen, The Earl of Westbrook and Lady Mira Brennen, The Countess of Westbrook. *Wait! What?* Catherine reread the sentence she had just read. "Earl of Westbrook?" *Garrett's father was an Earl?* So, Garrett wasn't merely a violinist. He was the son of a prominent man back in Ireland…the son of an Earl. The document said he was the only surviving son of Lord Brennen. Did that mean his father had died? *Poor Garrett,* thought Catherine, her heart constricting at the thought of Garrett's suffering. *That must be why he rushed off so quickly and returned home.*

Catherine was slowly putting the pieces together in her mind. *If Garrett's father has died and he is the only surviving son, then that means…Garrett is an…an* Earl? The paper slipped from Catherine's hand as that realization took hold.

Garrett was an Earl. But why had he never told her? Surely, he knew her aunt would have welcomed him as her niece's suitor had she known the truth. Why would he keep such a thing a secret?

Thinking back on their conversations, Catherine remembered the last time they had met on the terrace at Lord Harington's masquerade ball. Garrett had gone to great lengths to sneak into the ball to see her. Or had he? Had her husband already been made aware of Garrett's position at the time? Had he perhaps even invited him? No, she could never believe that Garrett would lie to her about how he'd come to be at the ball. Then again, he had most certainly kept secrets from her.

Catherine remembered that Garrett had said on the terrace that evening that he had something he wished to tell her, but their conversation had been cut short when they'd heard voices approaching. Then he had disappeared. And Catherine had never seen him again. Had he meant that night to reveal himself to Catherine? She had no way of knowing if that had been Garrett's intention or not. Of course, none of it mattered now anyway. He was back in Ireland, and she was here in England, a very recent widow still in mourning.

As Catherine's head began to clear, her thoughts returned to her husband. *Why had Brooks hired a private investigator to collect information on Garrett in the first place?* She wondered. *And how long had he been privy to the information within these documents?*

Catherine picked up the first page which contained the information that had been collected on Garrett's family. It was dated six months prior. So, Brooks had known about Garrett's true identity well before they'd married, even before he'd proposed to Catherine. And he'd been aware all along of her attraction to Garrett. So, if he was truly her friend as he'd claimed to be, why had he kept this information to himself when he'd come into possession of it? What reasoning could he have in keeping it from her?

Never believing her husband to be a devious man, Catherine could not, therefore, accept that he had withheld the information he'd received for deceitful purposes. As far as she could ascertain, there could only be one reason why Brooks would do such a thing. He loved her and had already made up his mind that he would ask her to marry him. He also knew that if she were made aware of Garrett's true circumstances, she would never have agreed to become his wife. So, he loved her, yes, she knew that much was true. But apparently, he was either very selfish in his love, or he did not love her enough to give her what would truly have made her most happy.

Feeling betrayed beyond measure, Catherine searched the file, reading through the other pages from Mr. Stirling's investigation. There were records of Garrett's birth, his academic records, notations relating to his musical prowess on the violin, and the record of his return to Ireland just before the death of his father.

Catherine perused the list of holdings in the Earl of Westbrook's possession, which all now apparently belonged to Garrett. There were numerous land holdings, many of which had passed from generation to generation for centuries. There had also been some wise investors in the family throughout the years, and a small fortune had been amassed. As the only direct male heir, Garrett now owned all of it.

None of it mattered now, though. Garrett was long gone, settled back in his homeland, a wealthy landowner and probably a husband and father by now as well. And Catherine was here in London, dressed in mourning attire, a young and wealthy widow with no interest in continuing on with her life. Indeed, she had wished on more than one occasion that it had been she and not Brooks who had perished in the carriage accident.

Catherine mourned not only the loss of her husband, but the loss of her true love, Garrett, as well. She mourned what could have been had she and Garrett been given the chance, the freedom, to embrace their love. Had she known the truth, Catherine would never have let go of her dream of having Garrett to love. She never would have settled for Brooks.

True, she had grown to love Brooks in the end, but it was not the same love she felt for Garrett. While he had treated her to pleasures she'd never dreamed of, Brooks' touch had never sent fiery flames through her entire body the way Garrett's touch had. While Brooks' kisses did elicit passion-filled responses from Catherine, they had never ignited her in the way Garrett's kiss had.

All this time, she'd thought Garrett hadn't wanted her, that he had left without telling her because he had not wanted to pursue any further dalliance with her. But it appeared the true reason behind his leaving so abruptly had been due to his father's ill health. Still, he had never returned. Perhaps he hadn't wanted Catherine after all. Perhaps he'd had someone back home in Ireland awaiting his return.

Despite lack of evidence, Catherine was convinced that Garrett had shared the same feelings for her that she had held, and continued to hold, for him. She did not believe it was possible to fake what had transpired between them in the brief moments they had shared.

And now to find that Brooks had betrayed her, that he had kept her from her true love and potential happiness for purely selfish reasons, Catherine's feelings for her deceased husband once again became a jumbled mess. It seemed Brooks wasn't the man Catherine had believed him to be after all. He had always touted honesty and openness, all the while keeping this huge secret from her.

Her poor heart was doubly broken as she mourned her losses, her what might have been, her happily ever after that would never come now. Crossing her arms on the desk, she rested her forehead against them, sobbing, as the overwhelming sadness overtook her.

Awaking with a start, and raising her head from the desk, Catherine glanced around the room. Had there been a noise? Perhaps not. She had been sleeping sporadically ever since her aunt had disposed of the laudanum. She rubbed her hands over her face. Her eyelids felt coated with sand, the result of her distraught tears after finding out the truth about Garrett and about

Brooks. She had no idea how long she'd slept. It was still dark outside. Hauling herself up from the desk chair, Catherine replaced the contents of the file, retying the leather strip. She then carried the file with her as she left the library and made her way up the stairs to her room. She would at least try to sleep a bit longer before the day crept upon her.

Catherine woke late the next morning feeling less than refreshed. She was still trying to absorb the information about Garrett that she had found among Brooks' legal documents the night before. Her emotions were a mass of confusion, hurt, anger, and disappointment. How could someone who claimed to have loved her do something so hurtful. She struggled with herself, trying to find a way to forgive Brooks for the hurt he had caused her.

It was too late now. There was nothing to be done to change the situation. She would have to find forgiveness in her heart for her dead husband and his actions if she wanted to move on with her life. And she would have to make peace as well with the fact that she would probably never see Garrett again. They had missed their chance at love and happiness.

What she needed was to purge herself of the past, pull herself out of this piteous state she'd grown so fond of, and make some new dreams, set new goals. She had been gifted with the opportunity and the financial security to do or become anything she wished. And she didn't need a man to give her the approval to pursue whatever she chose to do. Brooks had been very supportive of her in her pursuits, no matter how lofty they may have been, but she was now prepared to move forward with some of those endeavors.

Brooks had left Catherine more than well provided for. She found herself in possession of more wealth than she knew what to do with, and certainly more than she would ever need to sustain her own level of comfort. She made the decision to sell the massive London house as she had no desire to live there.

With the help of her husband's solicitor, Catherine used the money she received on the sale of the London mansion to purchase a large, plain, brick building on the outskirts of town and after much renovation, she opened a school of music in her late husband's name. The Brooks Academy of Music would be available to all who wished to pursue the study of music. She established the Catherine Darling Foundation which would provide scholarships for anyone wishing to attend the academy, regardless of their social standing. No one would ever be denied entrance to the school solely based on their level of income or social status.

Catherine enjoyed visiting the school whenever she was in London. It brought her great joy to see so many young people developing their musical talents. Yet, despite the pleasure it brought her whenever she visited, she always returned home feeling empty and bereft. For, during her visits to the school, she couldn't help but have her thoughts drift back to her own beloved violinist, Garrett.

Most days, she managed to keep herself busy enough that her mind remained focused on other things, household duties, gardening, reading, and such. But there were times when her early memories of the time spent with Garrett would demand her attention. It was during these moments that Catherine became quite melancholy and withdrawn. Usually, Abby was able to draw her out of her melancholy, but there were times when only a visit from her dear friend, Mary, would do the trick.

It did Catherine no good at all to dwell on the past. What was done was done and there was no going back. She must keep focused on the present and look toward the future. She must find other endeavors in which to invest her time and money.

Catherine found a small cottage on the outskirts of London that was to her liking and, once again enlisting help from the solicitor, she was able to purchase it. Once settled there, she retained the man further to help her choose some wise investments. Her fortunes continued to grow at a faster rate than she could dream possible, even with all of her benevolent donations to worthy causes and such.

She never traveled much, except to visit her aunt and few friends in London on occasion. She much preferred to stay at home, enjoying the peacefulness of her small garden and reading the many books she had brought with her from her late husband's library. This, she felt, was what held her together and helped her to keep her sanity in the months following her husband's death.

It had been well over a year since that fateful day. Her mourning period had ended months ago, though Catherine still wore her dark gowns and avoided any social gatherings. The London season was fast approaching, and this season, she would be expected to re-join in the activities of the *ton* as society warranted. She dreaded even the thought of such bothersome and, to her thinking, dull engagements. The idea of such gatherings, filled with nonsensical tittering and mindless conversation, made Catherine wish for a cave somewhere that she could retreat to and hide for the duration of the season. Her aunt, of course, would have none of that.

CHAPTER EIGHTEEN

"Ask not if still I love,
Too plain these eyes have told thee;
Too well their tears must prove
How near and dear I hold thee."
from *Ask Not If I Still Love*

Aunt Margaret invited Catherine to come and stay with her for the duration of the season. Though Catherine loved her aunt dearly, she knew that staying with her would mean an overwhelming number of social engagements she would be required to attend. Perhaps, with her aunt's support, she could overcome her anxieties and withstand the mundaneness (in her opinion anyway) of the London season. The upcoming dinner at Lord and Lady Hawthorne's would be her first social outing since her time of mourning had ended. Needless to say, she was not looking forward to it.

The evening of the dinner, Aunt Margaret insisted Catherine wear a new rose-colored gown with beautiful cream lace trimmings that she had ordered for her niece upon Catherine's acceptance to come and stay with her for the season. She refused to allow Catherine to leave the house in any of the dreary, dark gowns she had brought with her. She would take her niece shopping for more gaily colored gowns as soon as it could be arranged.

Catherine was a ball of nerves as they arrived at the Hawthorne's London home later that evening. She was not looking forward to an evening of forced conversation. This being her first outing since coming out of mourning, she was sure all attention would be on her, and she dreaded the thought of it. At least Lord and Lady Mosbey would be there as well. She hoped that seeing her friends would provide some relief.

Everyone was gathered in the front parlor when Catherine and Aunt Margaret entered. Catherine was pleased to find it was a small gathering. Lady Hawthorne came over to greet them as soon as she saw them. She gave Catherine a brief hug.

"My dear Catherine, it is so good to see you. We are so happy you are able to join us tonight." Her words seemed sincere and they immediately put Catherine more at ease. Though Catherine was not as well-known to Lord and Lady Hawthorne as her aunt was, she had been to their house on several occasions for both dinner parties and balls.

"Come ladies, we are just about to go in to dinner." Lady Hawthorne took Catherine's arm, leading her further into the room. "Of course, you know Lord and Lady Mosbey," she said as they approached the familiar couple. Lady Mosbey rose from her seat to embrace Catherine.

"It is so nice to see you, dear. You look absolutely lovely. I trust you are faring well?"

"Yes, my lady," replied Catherine. "I have been quite well. Thank you for asking. I hear from Anna that you will soon be welcoming your first grandchild."

"Oh yes, and I am beyond excited!" exclaimed Lady Mosbey. "I absolutely cannot wait to spoil the dear child." She let out a gleeful laugh, just as the butler appeared to announce that dinner was ready to be served. Lord Mosbey turned to his wife and Catherine.

"May I have the pleasure of escorting you lovely ladies into the dining room?" He held both arms out to them. Catherine placed her hand lightly on one arm while his wife took the other and they proceeded into the dining room. As it was a smaller gathering tonight, they were eating in the more intimate dining room rather than the large banquet room.

Lord Mosbey seated his wife, then turned to seat Catherine next to him. As she took her seat, she glanced about the table, taking notice of the other guests. A few of them were couples who were known to her, and there were several others whom she did not recognize.

Her gaze suddenly stilled when her eyes landed on a young gentleman seated at the right hand of their hostess, Lady Hawthorne, and next to her Aunt Margaret. He was quite handsome and well dressed in a wine-colored coat with an intricately tied, cream colored cravat. His dark locks hung loose around his collar, longer than most men wore their hair. She watched as he spoke with Lady Hawthorne.

As if sensing her attentions, the man suddenly turned toward her, and their eyes met. Catherine gasped. *No! Impossible! It couldn't be! What on earth was Garrett doing here*? Catherine's heart raced as they continued to stare at one another. He seemed as stunned as she felt. His eyes first widened in surprise, then clouded with something Catherine couldn't quite make out. Was it sadness she saw there?"

Next to her, Lord Mosbey became aware of Catherine's attention toward the young man and smiled. Leaning closer to her, he whispered. "I see our young Lord Westbrook has captured your attention." Patting her arm, he continued. "No worries, my dear. I shall introduce you after we've dined."

"That won't be necessary, my lord," said Catherine, finding her voice. "We are already well acquainted, though it has been quite some time since we last spoke."

"Wonderful!" Lord Mosbey gushed, taking up his fork and beginning to eat with gusto. "Then you shall have some catching up to do after the meal. I hear Lord Westbrook has agreed to entertain us with some music afterwards as well. That should be a treat."

A treat, indeed, thought Catherine. She was barely able to keep her thoughts on the task of eating and contributed very little in the way of conversation as the meal progressed. It took every bit of her concentration to keep her gaze from continually returning to Garrett. She caught him looking at her several times and wondered what thoughts could be going through his head. She didn't know whether to look forward to a later encounter with him or to feign a headache and retreat as soon as dinner ended.

Her aunt seemed to be quite interested in conversing with him, which astonished Catherine. On one occasion, Catherine spied them both looking her way, Garrett with a secret smile, and her aunt with a pleased look on her face.

After the meal, the ladies gathered briefly back in the parlor as the men were ushered into the library for a glass of port and (for those who indulged) a cigar. After just a few moments, Garrett excused himself and made his way to the music room next door to prepare himself for the few musical pieces he had agreed to perform for the group at Lady Hawthorne's request. Seeing Catherine had given him quite a shock and he needed a few moments to calm himself.

In the parlor, Aunt Margaret cornered Catherine. Fearing an admonishment, Catherine focused her eyes on the floor.

"That young Lord Westbrook is quite something, Catherine. Very handsome and most charming," she gushed. Bewildered, Catherine was at a loss as to how to respond. However, she needn't have worried as her aunt gave no pause in which for her to place a response. "And...he is an *Earl*," her aunt whispered enthusiastically. "I think I should introduce the two of as soon as possible." Lady Hathaway was positively giddy and flushed with excitement.

What is she about? wondered Catherine as the ladies made their way to the music room for Garrett's performance. *Surely, her opinion of him could not be so changed after just one conversation.*

As the guests began to file in and find seats in the large room, Garrett glanced up in time to see Lady Hathaway directing her niece to the front of the room. They seated themselves a mere few feet from where he stood. How would he ever manage to play a note with Catherine so near?

The guests were all seated, waiting patiently for him to begin. He risked a quick glance in Catherine's direction. Her eyes were focused on her hand which lay fidgeting in her lap. She did not look up. Placing the violin upon his shoulder, Garrett closed his eyes and began to play. He concentrated on the music and soon was able to block out all else as the music enveloped him. He moved effortlessly into the next piece and continued playing for some time.

When he'd finished the second composition, he gave a slight bow to his audience and noticed that Catherine looked about the room, anywhere but at him. Knowing it would surely draw her attention, he began to play "Lady Greensleeves." This time he did not close his eyes but watched closely for Catherine's reaction. As the first few notes resonated about the room, Catherine slowly lifted her eyes to meet his.

Garrett played the song slowly, mournfully, the bow caressing the strings in such a way it almost seemed as though the instrument itself was weeping. Through the music, he spoke to her, pleaded with her to forgive him, to put the past behind them and find a way to start again.

In her mind, Catherine heard the words to the song and couldn't help but compare them to her and Garret's own situation.

"Alas, my love, you do me wrong
to cast me off discourteously,
for I have loved you well and long,
delighting in your company.

Greensleeves was all my joy.
Greensleeves was my delight.
Greensleeves was my heart of god
and who but my lady Greensleeves?

Your vows you've broken, like my heart.
Oh, why did you so enrapture me?
Now I remain in a world apart
But my heart remains in captivity

Catherine's heart broke into pieces all over again as she watched Garrett playing. She knew he had chosen that song specifically for her, for this occasion. She knew he was begging her for forgiveness and making his feelings known to her through the music as well as in the unsung lyrics to the song. Barely breathing, she could not take her eyes from his as he played. Nor could he remove his gaze from hers.

By the time he reached the end of the piece, Catherine had tears streaming down her face. Thankful that she sat in the front row and most of the guests wouldn't have been able to see her tears, she rose from her seat and, mumbling a low, "Please excuse me," to her aunt and the guests nearby, she exited the room and quickly as possible.

A few of the guests gasped at her abrupt departure, curious as to what had caused such unseemly behavior on her part. They became even more aghast when Garrett quickly finished the tune, set down his instrument and, making his apologies, hastily exited the room as well.

Reaching the front entrance, Catherine called to the footman to bring her carriage. "Quickly, please."

Seeing the young women's distress, he hurried off to do as she'd asked.

Catherine, unable to bear pacing back and forth in the foyer while she waited, took a step toward the door.

"Lady Harington…Catherine…please…wait."

Catherine halted her steps, the familiar voice embracing her as if it were a physical thing. Slowly, she turned to face the man whose arms had once caressed her as well as his endearing words, but she made no move to bridge the space between them.

Meeting his gaze squarely, Catherine spoke softly. "Why didn't you tell me the truth about who you were?" Pain, disappointment, and accusation all gathered in her eyes.

Garrett's hand reached toward her of its own accord. He stilled it though every part of his being ached to touch her. His eyes pleaded with her for forgiveness and understanding.

"I tried to tell you." His soft tone matched Catherine's. "The last time we met...on the terrace, at the masquerade. I was prepared to confess everything to you, but you will recall we were interrupted by other guests approaching the terrace."

Catherine nodded slightly, remembering. "You disappeared," she stated plainly.

"It wasn't by choice," he said. Garrett paused, his thoughts drifting back to the night of the masquerade. He'd left the terrace quickly and quietly when they'd heard the voices approaching, not wanting to expose Catherine to the judgment and condemnation of others who might find them there in a compromising situation.

As Garrett had stepped away from the terrace that night and into the surrounding darkness, a movement in the shadows caught his attention. The figure of a man stepped toward him just as strong hands grabbed hold of his arms from behind. Two strong men held him. Garrett struggled against their stronghold as Lord Darling approached him.

"Mister...Brennen, isn't it?" Lord Harington asked casually. He didn't wait for a reply. "Funny, I don't recall inviting you to my ball, Mr. Brennen. And yet, here you are."

Garrett glared at him, saying nothing. Brooks glared back. "Tell me, what is a violinist doing at my masquerade if he is not playing a violin? Ah, but you are not merely a violinist, are you, *Lord* Rathburn?"

Knowing he could not give a satisfactory answer, Garrett kept quiet.

"Very well, you need not answer," Brooks said, stepping closer to Garrett. "I know who you are Rathburn, and I also know why you are here. You've set your sights on Catherine Elmsworth, have you not?" His eyes hardened. Leaning in close to Garrett's face, Brooks sneered. "You will never have her, Rathburn. I plan to see to that." Straightening, his voice again taking on a casual, polite tone, he said, "Now, I must insist you leave my property immediately." With a slight nod to the men holding Garrett, he added, "and do not attempt to return or I will be forced to resort to more drastic measures."

Shaking his head to rid it of the memory, Garrett eyes held Catherine's. It was time she knew the truth about the kind of man she'd married. Garrett cleared his throat and began.

"When I left the terrace that night, I was met by Lord Harington and two other men. As the men held me, Harington insisted I leave his property immediately. He then issued a threat should I ever return." Garrett watched as confusion clouded Catherine's features.

"He knew my true identity, Catherine. He also knew of my attraction to you, and he swore he would see to it that I would never have you."

Silence hung between them as Catherine took in all that Garrett had told her. She barely heard his next words.

"The next morning, I received word from my mother of my father's illness. She bid me come home quickly. I left immediately."

Garrett watched as a single tear spilled from Catherine's eye and slid down her cheek. It took all of his self-control to keep from reaching out to wipe it away.

"But…you never came back," she whispered.

Garrett took another step toward her. With earnest, he replied, "I did come back, Catherine. As soon as my father's affairs were set in order, I came back to London to see you, to tell you everything." His gaze and his voice filled with longing, he said, "I came back to ask for your hand in marriage."

Her confused gaze met his. "I don't understand," she said. "If you came back, why was I not aware of it? Why did you not come for me, Garrett?"

"You never knew of my return because you were in Paris at the time…on your honeymoon." He kept to himself the angry accusation that ate at his heart. That it was she, not him, who had not waited.

Clarity dawned fully on Catherine's face as all the pieces fell into place. Once again her husband, whom she had trusted, had betrayed her by keeping the truth from her. Because of him, she had been denied the chance to be with the man she truly loved.

She looked at Garrett. "I've been such a fool," she cried. "Can you ever forgive me, Garrett?" Her eyes pleading, she searched his for some sign that he might still carry some fondness for her.

Stepping forward, Garrett took Catherine's hands in his. "Catherine," he said, his voice trembling. "There is no need for forgiveness, my love. We have both been wronged, not of our own choosing, by a man who acted wrongly only out of his own love for you. I cannot truthfully say that I would not have done the same thing had our roles been reversed."

Catherine's tears flowed freely now. "But, I should have waited. I should have trusted that you would return."

Garrett could restrain himself no longer. Taking Catherine in his arms, he held her tightly until her tears subsided. He pulled back from her, so that he could see her face. Wiping away her tears, he held her face in his hands. "Dearest Catherine, I am here now, and you are here. We are here together, now, and that is all that matters."

Hearing a commotion approaching, they quickly drew apart. Aunt Margaret came rushing into the hallway, followed closely by Ladies Hawthorne and Mosbey. Her momentum halted abruptly when she saw the two of them together, guilt flushing both their faces.

"What goes on here?" she asked accusingly. When no answer was immediate, she turned first to Catherine, then to Garrett, and back again.

"Catherine," she beseeched, "What is the meaning of this?"

Sensing a need to form some kind of feasible answer, Catherine went to her aunt and, grasping both of Margaret's plump hands in her own, she looked (she hoped sincerely) into her aunt's eyes.

"Aunt Margaret, please do not fret. Lord Westbrook came upon me in my distressed state and was only trying to offer me some solace." She glanced discreetly back at Garrett.

Stepping forward, Garrett added, "I can assure you nothing untoward happened, Lady Hathaway. I merely sought assurance that Lady Harington was all right."

Eyeing them both warily, she seemed to accept their explanation as a smile began to form on her lips and Catherine could swear there was even a small glint that appeared in her eyes. Reaching to take Garrett's hand, Lady Margaret said, "Lord Brennen, Earl of Westbrook, may I formally introduce you to my niece, Lady Catherine Darling, Countess of Harington?"

Realizing that Lady Hathaway had no idea that the lord standing before her was the very same young violin player she had forbidden to ever see her niece, Catherine and Garrett both bit back smiles and tried willfully to put on a sober face as they pretended to be meeting for the first time.

Taking her hand lightly in his, Garrett bowed slightly, his eyes never leaving hers. "Lady Harington, may I say it is my utmost pleasure to have your dear aunt introduce us."

Laughter about to burst forth from her, Catherine literally bit her tongue to keep herself focused on the seriousness of the moment at hand.

"Lord Westbrook," she answered, keeping her eyes low. She knew if she looked at Garrett, it would be her undoing. "I assure you, the pleasure is mine."

Spying their carriage approaching, Lady Hathaway stepped around the two young people, saying as she went, "Well, now that that is done with, perhaps, Catherine, it is time you and I departed, as our carriage is already here."

Turning back, she thanked Lady Hawthorne for a lovely evening and bid both her and Lady Mosbey a goodnight, before climbing into the carriage. Seating herself, she urged Catherine, "Come along, dear."

Garrett held out a hand to aid Catherine into the carriage. Once she was seated, he closed the carriage door. Though he said nothing, his eyes held Catherine's as he bid both ladies good evening.

"Do come and pay us a visit, Lord Westbrook," Margaret suddenly spoke. "You are welcome any time, young man."

Face serious, Garrett nodded slightly in acknowledgement of the offer. "Thank you, Lady Hathaway. I mean to take you up on that offer." Smiling, he took a step back as the carriage began to move.

Two agonizing days later, Garrett called on Lady Hathaway and Catherine. After half an hour of polite conversation, he turned to Lady Hathaway.

"Lady Hathaway, I wonder if you would mind terribly if I were to take your niece out for a walk?"

Smiling broadly, Aunt Margaret beamed at him. "Why, of course not, my lord. It is the perfect weather outside for a walk."

Ringing for Abby to bring Catherine's shawl and bonnet, Margaret ushered the young couple toward the front entrance.

"You two go on, now, and enjoy yourselves."

Moments later, Catherine and Garrett found themselves nearly pushed out the door. With a chuckle, Garrett held out his arm. "'Tis a lovely day for a walk, is it not, lass?"

Smiling up at him, Catherine took his arm. They walked in silence for a few moments.

"Do you think she'll ever figure it out?" asked Catherine.

"Perhaps," Garrett answered, grinning down at her. "But by then, she will be so enamored of me, I'm sure she won't mind a whit."

Giggling, Catherine argued, "Perhaps we should tell her the truth before she finds out from some other source."

"If you insist, my dear, but not before I've asked her for your hand in marriage," he said casually.

"What-?"

Catherine's response was cut short when Garrett brought his lips to hers with a soft kiss.

Pushing away from him, Catherine gasped, "Garrett! People will see." Her eyes darted around, searching for prying eyes.

Grasping her hand, he tried to calm her. "Relax, my love, 'tis nothing to bother about. What does it matter if anyone were to pass by and see a betrothed couple engaging in a brief show of affection."

"Garrett," She began.

His heart swelled as her eyes, so full of love, looked up into his. He had waited so long for this moment. Releasing her, he took a step back and fell to one knee as he took her hand in his.

"Catherine, no one else could ever lay claim to my heart as you have. Please allow me the honor of proving my love to you, from this day forward, by becoming my wife."

"Yes," she cried. "Yes, of course. Nothing would make me happier, my love."

Rising, Garrett bowed formally with a gleam in his eye, entreating, "Permit me to escort you home, my lady. There is an urgent matter I need to discuss with your aunt."

Placing her hand at his elbow, Catherine held in a grin, as they made their way back to Aunt Margaret's.

"You are aware she might say 'no'?" Catherine teased.

Garrett shook his head in serious disagreement. "I have every confidence she will say 'yes' without a moment's hesitation."

"And if she doesn't?" Catherine prodded.

"Then I will have to increase my efforts to assure her that I am the very best man to entrust her niece's future well-being to."

Catherine burst out laughing. "I wish you great luck in that endeavor, my lord."

As they approached the house, Garrett could not keep the smile from his face.

"I believe it is going to be great fun being married to you, Catherine," he said with a grin.

"Wonderful!" Catherine responded with glee. "It is high time we both had a bit of fun, don't you agree?"

"Aye, that I do, lass, that I do."

ABOUT THE AUTHOR

Kimberly Westrope grew up in Phoenix, AZ and has been writing since elementary school. She has two grown sons and two beautiful grandchildren. She lives in Southern California.

The Earl's Masquerade is Kimberly's second published novel, and her first Regency romance. She has also published an Inspirational romance, *Brother's* Keeper, and two books of poetry, *Dancing On Borders*, a collection of love poems, and *The Prints of All My Days,* poems about life, love, and other things.

The Earl's Masquerade

Before you go…

If you enjoyed this book, please consider leaving a brief review on Amazon, Goodreads, or another website where you purchased the book.

The best way to show an author some love, other than buying and reading their books, of course, is to leave a positive review of the book.

Even if you don't have a few words to say about why you liked the book, you can still leave a rating.

I would very much appreciate it. Thank you in advance.

I would also love to hear from you.

You can contact me at
kimberly.westrope@gmail.com

https://www.facebook.com/kimberly.westrope.5

http://kimberlywestropeauthor.wordpress.com/

www.ingramcontent.com/pod-product-compliance
Lightning Source LLC
Chambersburg PA
CBHW072205170626
46813CB00003B/793